DIANA
THE HUNTRESS

Also available in Large Print
by Marion Chesney:

Daphne
Deirdre and Desire
The Taming of Annabelle
Minerva

DIANA
THE HUNTRESS

Marion Chesney

G.K.HALL&CO.
Boston, Massachusetts
1986

Published in Large Print by arrangement with
St. Martin's Press.

G.K. Hall Large Print Book Series.

Set in 16 pt Plantin.

Library of Congress Cataloging in Publication Data

Chesney, Marion.
  Diana the huntress.

  (G.K. Hall large print book series)
  1. Large type books. I. Title.
[PR6053.H4535D5 1986]   823'.914   85-27180
ISBN 0-8161-3997-0 (lg. print)

For Harry Scott Gibbons
and
Charles David Bravos Gibbons

With love.

HONEST JOHN BULL

Here's a health to 'Old honest John Bull',
When he's gone we shan't find such another;
With hearts and with glasses brim full,
We'll drink to 'Britania, his mother,'
For she gave him a good education,
Bade him keep to his God and his King,
Be loyal and true to the nation,
And then to get merry and sing.

For John is a good-natured fellow,
Industrious, honest and brave;
Not afraid of his better when mellow,
For betters he knows he must have.
There must be fine lords and fine ladies,
There must be some little, some great;
Their wealth the support of our trade is,
Our trade the support of the State.

The plough and the loom would stand still,
If we were made gentlefolks all;
If clodhoppers—who then would fill

The parliament, pulpit or hall?
'Rights of Man' makes a very fine sound,
'Equal riches' a plausible tale;
Whose labourers would then till the ground?
All would drink, but who'd brew the ale?

Half naked and starv'd in the streets,
We would wander about, *sans culottes;*
Would Liberty find us in meats,
Or Equality lengthen our coats?
That knaves are for levelling, don't wonder,
We may easily guess at their views;
Pray, who'd gain the most by the plunder?
Why, they that have nothing to lose.

The Norfolk Minstrel

CHAPTER ONE

Had she not had four extremely beautiful elder sisters, Diana Armitage might have been accounted very well in her way. She had heavy black hair and enormous dark eyes and a pale golden skin. But she affected mannish airs and lacked the charm and delicacy of her sisters and so was considered something of a cuckoo in the Armitage nest.

Her father, the vicar of St Charles and St Jude in the village of Hopeworth, the Reverend Charles Armitage, had devoted his life to the hunt rather than to the spiritual well-being of his parishioners. Such was his obsession with the sport that he allowed Diana to hunt—provided she dressed as a man—a disgraceful state of affairs which suited the gypsy-like Diana very well. It was a well-kept secret. Diana, in a buckram-wadded coat to hide her generous bosom and with her tresses pushed up under a hard hat, acquired all the grace and ease of movement

1

she lacked in the drawing room. Mrs Armitage, her mother, was prey to imaginary ills and mostly kept to her bedchamber, and was therefore not aware of the scandalous behaviour of her daughter.

Diana's four elder sisters had all married well. Minerva had married Lord Sylvester Comfrey; Annabelle, the Marquess of Brabington; Deirdre, Lord Harry Desire, and Daphne, Mr Simon Garfield.

Frederica, the youngest of the Armitage girls, had become a quiet, wispy, bookish thing. No one paid much attention to *her*. But Diana was so robust, so wild, and so terribly bad-mannered and gauche that it was hard to feel comfortable about her future. The vicar was torn between admiration for his daughter's prowess on the hunting field and fear for her future, although he tried to console himself with the thought that four well-married daughters was enough.

The twins, Peregrine and James, would soon be going up to Oxford. Boys were never any trouble and, if they got into a scrape, that was only to be expected.

Diana visited her married sisters as little as possible. She complained that they were always trying to marry her off to some 'Bond

Street Fribble', and did not know how often and how furiously her sisters, especially Minerva, wrote to the vicar to beg papa to let Diana come to town for an extended period so that she could at least get the smell of the stables out of her clothes.

Perhaps the vicar might have paid heed had he not become consumed with ambition to hunt down an old grey dog fox which had been making his life a misery for the past few years. Try as he would, the vicar could never catch the beast and often thought the old fox was the devil himself come to mock him.

Diana had been invaluable during cub-hunting where the young hounds were taught to hunt the fox with the older dog-hounds and bitches.

That cold November day, he was to ride over to the other side of Hopeminster to pay a call on Mr and Mrs Chumley, friends of his son-in-law, Mr Garfield. The vicar planned to go hunting on the morrow, and to ease his conscience he was first taking Diana on a social call. To see Diana struck dumb by polite company always eased the vicar's conscience. The girl was only at home on the hunting field. So why not let her hunt! It was not as if any of the local county knew that the handsome young man who hunted alongside the vicar was his daughter. Even old Squire Radford did not know, and the squire was the vicar's oldest and closest friend.

The old dog fox had not been seen in the neighbourhood for some time until two days ago, and the vicar had been up early destroying every earth and every place that a fox might get into. He returned to the vicarage to change his muddy clothes and prepare to go out with Diana to call on the Chumleys. The dark silence of the vicarage hit him afresh. Not so long ago, when all the girls were at home—and the twins—there seemed to be a constant coming and going.

Now the rooms seemed smaller and darker. Mrs Armitage had just tried some new purge to cleanse the blood, and the results had been so violent that she was now prostrate abovestairs being administered to by the maid, Sarah. Frederica was in the parlour, curled up on the window seat with her head in a book. Her once curly hair now surrounded her pinched little face in wisps.

'Where is Diana?' asked the vicar.

Frederica looked at him with large,

drowned eyes and slowly put a finger on the page to mark her place.

'Dressing, Papa,' she said, looking at him beseechingly. The vicar knew that look of old. It meant, 'Please do go away and leave me to my book.'

'Go and find Sarah and send her to me immediately,' snapped the vicar.

Frederica sighed and put down her book and drifted from the room as if floating under water.

Betty, who had acted as lady's maid to the four elder sisters, was now happily married to the coachman, John Summer. The vicar was still parsimonious when it came to engaging servants and so although Sarah was lady's maid, she was also parlour maid and chaperone. John Summer was still groom, kennel master and whipper-in as well as coachman.

Sarah came tripping in and the vicar eyed her in the sort of way no gentleman, least of all a vicar, should eye one of his servants. There was no denying that Sarah was a full-blown country rose. Her blonde hair gleamed with health and her impertinent breasts thrust out gloriously against her apron. The vicar's little shoe-button eyes gleamed appreciatively in his round face and he tried to pull in his stomach.

'What's Miss Diana wearing?' he demanded.

Sarah giggled. 'Miss Diana is wearing that old purple gown she always wears when she is going calling, sir.'

'Well, see here, miss, you go upstairs direct and tell that daughter of mine she's to wear the muslin Minerva sent her and that pelisse thing, *and* the new bonnet that goes with it or I'll take the whip to her. Run along with you.'

Sarah giggled again and tossed her head so that the jaunty little streamers on her cap flicked the vicar on the face.

The vicar followed her out. He had to change himself and, besides, watching Sarah mount the stairs was a sight not to be missed.

His stomach rumbled. He never could get used to these newfangled hours. They would reach the Chumleys by four in the afternoon, which was the time any civilized creature should be sitting down to dinner. But the Chumleys kept London hours, and so he would get nothing but tea. His breakfast of beef steak and porter, oysters, bread and butter, eggs, muffins, prawns and fried ham seemed a long time ago.

He fished in the cupboard under the toilet table, where he kept his bottle of moon-shine—smuggled white brandy—and took a hearty pull. He began to dream about the following day's hunting. Surely he would catch that fox at last and prove to himself that it was no supernatural being, but vermin like all the others.

He drank and dreamed, and dreamed and drank, only suddenly becoming aware of the time when Sarah scratched at the door and called out that Miss Diana was belowstairs, waiting for him.

He finished his toilet in a scrambled rush, crammed his shovel hat on his head, and made his way downstairs. Sarah rushed to hold open the parlour door for him.

For one moment, the vicar thought the elegant lady in front of him was a stranger. Then he realized it was indeed Diana. But what a transformation!

Her black hair curled from under the smartest of bonnets, the brim lined with wine-coloured silk. Her muslin gown was of pale gold, embroidered with sheaves of corn and wild flowers and tied under her bosom with two long satin ribbons. Her pelisse was of the same burgundy colour as her bonnet.

The clever choice of colours set off the honey of her skin. When she was in repose, with her strong tanned hands hidden by doeskin gloves and with her large mouth—too large for beauty—softened by dreams and her enormous eyes veiled yet sparkling like wisps of cloud crossing the starry sky at night, there was something about her that was beyond the beauty of her elder sisters.

Then the spell was broken. Diana became aware of her father watching her and said harshly, 'Shall we go, Papa? As soon as this call is over and done with, I shall be glad to return to a more civilized form of dress.'

'More uncivilized, you mean,' said the vicar sourly. 'You cannot claim that what you are wearing is uncomfortable.'

'Not indoors in front of the fire, Papa. Outside, I shall probably freeze to death. Are you taking your racing curricle?'

'Of course.'

'Then I hope the Chumleys like the sight of blue ladies. Oh, do I have to go, Papa? I am persuaded they will not like me.'

'And if they do, you will soon make sure

that they don't,' grumbled the vicar. 'Soon as you're in the drawing room, you seem to delight in behaving in as uncouth a manner as possible. Come along, then.'

Diana followed her father from the vicarage. She wondered if she told her father the real reason for her gauche behaviour in society, whether he would understand.

For the fact was that Diana Armitage was painfully shy anywhere off the hunting field. She feared men, she admired them, she longed to be one. Social behaviour was a genteel prison. There was no freedom of speech. One had to be gratified by everything that happened, whether it was a pleasure or a pain. She pulled the rugs tightly about her as they set off down the Hopeminster road.

The vicar slowed his team as they came abreast of the small figure of Squire Radford walking along the road beside the village pond. The squire waved his arm, signalling the vicar to stop.

Squire Radford removed his old-fashioned tricorne and bowed from the waist.

'You are in looks, Miss Diana,' he said. 'Do you go to the Chumleys, Charles?'

'Yes, Jimmy. Bit o' company for Diana.'

'The reason I stopped you,' said the squire in his high, precise voice, 'is because I have a desire to hunt with you tomorrow.'

'Wouldn't do that, Jimmy,' said the vicar hurriedly, thinking of Diana's masquerade. 'Bound to be uncommon sharp. Bad weather for old bones.'

'So is a sedentary life,' smiled the squire. 'Expect me on the morrow, Charles.' He bowed again. The vicar impatiently flapped the reins.

'Well, here's a problem,' said the vicar when they had bowled along some distance out of Hopeworth village. 'Can't go hunting tomorrow, Diana. Not with Jimmy Radford's sharp old eyes on you.'

Unshed tears of frustration filmed Diana's dark eyes. But, unlike her sisters, she did not trouble to argue with the vicar. The answer would be 'no', no matter what she said. Some way or other she would go.

But Diana, who had been secretly pleased with her new fashionable appearance and who had planned to be as feminine as possible at the Chumleys in order to please her father, now decided to be as awful as possible.

When people retreated from you in

disgust, they left you alone. And if being alone was a rather miserable state of affairs, there was always the consolation of being left in peace to dream of the next day's hunting. Diana had no interest in the kill. Only in the thrill of fast, often dangerous, hard exercise.

Diana still remembered her first ride in the way other, more genteel misses, remembered their first love. She had taken out one of her father's hunters and had ridden off, sailing across stone walls, across little brooks, over flat fields with her hair streaming out behind her, drunk with freedom, only returning when the light was fading, shaken all over and practically unable to move hand or foot for a week and never once regretting a moment of it.

They reached the crossroads, Diana closing her eyes until they were safely past. For suicides were buried at crossroads, and superstitious Diana was sure their ghosts walked even during the day. When she opened her eyes, the sun was piercing through a bank of angry black clouds, great shafts of yellow light, the kind that angels ascend and descend in the Bible pictures.

The vicar muttered something under his breath and the curricle rolled to a stop.

11

Beside the road, two or three lean ponies were cropping the grass. A little way into a small wood stood a shabby tent with smoke curling out of it, a light cart at its side.

'Egyptians,' grumbled the vicar. 'Bad cess to 'em. Hey! You!' he shouted, climbing down from the curricle and striding forward.

A woman emerged from the tent. Her coarse hair hung down to her waist. She wore a low bodice and a dirty petticoat and her skin was dark and swarthy.

'Where is your man?' demanded the vicar.

'Oh, delicate Jesus, your honour,' said the gypsy woman with an odd bobbing curtsey. 'Gone I know not where.'

'And you won't say so either, will you?' snorted the vicar. 'Gone to steal hens, heh! Tell him that Charles Armitage says you must be gone by sundown.'

The woman's eyes flashed and she began to mutter something in a strange tongue. The vicar strode back to the curricle and mounted, ignoring the stream of incomprehensible Romany directed at his back.

Diana stared in terror. She had heard of the gypsies, but had never seen any near Hopeworth before. Surely this terrifying-looking woman was a witch.

As the vicar picked up the reins, the gypsy came running up and put a filthy hand on the side of the carriage.

'You leave us stay and I'll tell the little lady's fortune,' she whined.

'Stand back!' said the vicar, raising his whip.

Diana tried to tear her eyes away from the gypsy woman but found she could not.

'Your lover will come soon, missie,' cackled the gypsy. 'He is tall and black and hunts the fox like yourself.'

The vicar's brandishing of the whip became more threatening and the gypsy turned and fled.

'A pox on those 'gyptians,' grumbled the vicar.

'And yet, I have heard it said, papa, that they have the art to foretell the future,' said Diana. 'No one else knows I go foxhunting but yourself and John Summer. How did she know?'

'Guessing,' snorted the reverend. 'And what's this rubbish about a tall, black lover? She was probably thinking of one of their own kind. Black as pitch they are, what with the smoke from their fires and their detestation of washing.'

13

Diana felt sick with nerves and an odd growing feeling of excitement. She privately believed every word the gypsy woman had said. All the terrible business of having a Season and getting married horrified Diana, since trapping a husband meant giggling and being missish and wearing such uncomfortable clothes. A *man* would never dream of wearing thin muslin on such a freezing day. But what if there was a gentleman waiting for her, someone who loved the chase as much as she did herself, and who would not be appalled by the fact that she hunted?

Diana passed the rest of the journey in a happy dream, and by the time they reached the Chumleys she was convinced that some huntsman was waiting to fall in love with her.

But the Chumleys had only two other guests and both of them were ladies, a Mrs Carter and her daughter, Ann.

The Chumleys were both small, round and placid. Mrs Carter was terrifyingly mondaine and had a long thin nose which seemed to have been expressly designed for looking down on lesser mortals. Her daughter, Ann, was a tiny porcelain shepherdess with blonde curls and wide blue eyes and little dimpled hands. Made clumsy and gauche by the cold looks of Mrs Carter, Diana upset her teacup and Ann gave a little cry of distress and shrank back from her, making Diana suddenly feel like some overgrown country yokel.

The Reverend Charles Armitage seemed delighted with the fairy-like Ann. It transpired that the Carters had just recently moved into the Hopeminster neighbourhood.

'You must call on us,' said the vicar to Mrs Carter. 'My little Diana has been languishing for some female company with her sisters all being wed, 'cept Frederica who don't count, being too young and bookish.'

He leered at Mrs Carter and leaned slightly towards her, exuding a strong smell of ammonia, damp dog, white brandy and musk.

Mrs Carter shuddered slightly and raised a little white handkerchief to her nostrils. She did not want to have anything to do with this boorish vicar and his uncouth daughter. But, on the other hand, all the world knew of the splendid marriages of the elder Armitage sisters, and friendship between Ann and Diana would mean social advantages for Ann when she made her come-out the following April.

'We should be delighted,' she said, bestowing a wintry smile on Diana who was staring at the clock in an anguished way, as if willing the hands to go faster.

'I am thinking of puffing Diana off at the next Season,' said the vicar, ignoring Diana's look of shock. 'Husbands ain't growing as thick around these parts as they used to.'

'Yes, indeed,' said Mrs Carter, raising her thin eyebrows in disapproval as Miss Diana, forgetting her manners, *crossed her legs.* The vicar followed Mrs Carter's gaze and kicked Diana under the tea table. Diana yelled 'ouch!' and glared defiantly at her father. The Reverend Charles Armitage sighed. Why was it that a girl like Diana could master the 'don'ts' of the hunting field so well—don't allow your horses to kick a hound, don't ride over a newly sown field, don't let stock out of the fields—and yet not seem to be able to remember one single social law?

'I think Berham county is not entirely bereft of eligible men,' giggled Ann. 'There is Lord Dantrey, of course.'

'No one has seen the young lord yet,' put in Mrs Chumley. 'He has taken

Osbadiston's place.'

'Poor Osbadiston,' mourned the vicar, tears starting to his eyes. 'Died in debt and did not even leave an heir. What a man he was. And what horseflesh he did have before the gambling brought him low. Who is this Dantrey fellow?'

Mrs Carter gave a superior laugh. 'I should have thought your married daughter would have put you to the wise. Lord Dantrey is reputed to be very rich and clever. He has been abroad much of his life and has only recently returned to this country. We are all anxious to make his acquaintance. The poor man must be dying of boredom. 'Tis said he sees no one.'

Diana made a great effort. 'Is this Lord Dantrey tall and dark?' she asked.

'I do not know,' said Mrs Carter frostily. 'Like many other hostesses of note in Berham county, I have sent him invitations but he has refused them all, albeit in a most courteous and civilized manner as befits his rank.'

'I'll send him a card,' said the vicar. 'He's bound to see me 'cos I'm better connected to the peerage than anyone else hereabouts. Found good husbands for my other

17

daughters. No harm in trying to catch the prize for Diana, heh!'

Mrs Carter's cold eyes took in Diana's sulky expression and awkward movements and then she smiled as her gaze turned to rest on her daughter. There was no one in the whole of Berham county who could compete with Ann Carter.

Under her china-doll exterior, Ann was thinking furiously. She did not like Diana. Nor, for that matter, did she like anyone of her own age and sex. But this Diana was related by her sisters' marriage to a top section of the ton. If this ugly little John Bull of a prelate could lure the mysterious Lord Dantrey to his table, then Ann planned to be present when he called.

She reached forward a little hand and squeezed Diana's larger one with a pretty show of impulsive warmth. 'Oh, do let us be friends, Miss Diana,' she said. 'I do so long for a friend.'

Diana looked down at the pretty Ann with a sudden rush of affection. No other girl had ever volunteered to call Diana 'friend'.

'I should like that above all things,' she said.

And Diana smiled. A wide enchanting

smile that lit up her face, turning that face, which only a moment before had been sulky and lowering, into a bewitching blaze of beauty.

Had Mrs Carter not been reaching forward to take another slice of Madeira cake, had she seen the transformed Diana, her daughter's proposal of friendship with Diana Armitage would have been quickly nipped in the bud. But, as it was, by the time she raised her eyes, the shadows of social embarrassment were once more clouding Diana's face and she looked as if she could never, under any circumstances, be competition to the fair Ann.

At last the visit was over. The wind had veered round to the west and by the time Mr Armitage and his daughter reached home, the rain was beginning to fall.

'Papa,' said Diana earnestly. 'Before we go indoors, I beseech you to let me ride on the morrow. Squire Radford will not recognize me.'

'He's the only person that would,' snorted the little vicar. 'Jimmy Radford may be old, but his eyes are as sharp as a hawk's. No, Diana. You'd best stay home and try to learn some pretty manners like that young Ann

Carter. Husband hunting's your sport from now on.'

'I do not want to get married,' said Diana passionately. 'I will never get married.'

But as she climbed the narrow stairs to her room, the words of the gypsy woman sounded in her ears.

In a coffee house in Hopeminster, Jack Emberton put one booted foot up on the low stool opposite and addressed his friend, Peter Flanders.

'On the subject of the ladies, Peter, I saw a deuced fine wench this day.'

'Silver or brass?' demanded Mr Flanders laconically.

'Oh, silver, definitely. Sat up behind some spanking bays with a little vicar.'

'Ah, that'd be one of the famous Armitage gels.'

A silence fell between the friends. Jack Emberton was tall and broad-shouldered, with a head of black curls and bright blue eyes set in a square, handsome, tanned face. Peter Flanders was tall, but thin and bony, his thinness accentuated by a tightly buttoned black coat worn over tight pantaloons which ended in long, thin, tight boots. He had a long, thin, tight face to go with the rest of him. His brown hair was back-combed into a crest on top of his head.

'Rich, ain't they? The Armitages, that is,' said Jack Emberton at last.

'Reverend ain't got a feather to fly with,' replied Mr Flanders, 'but his sons-in-law are all as rich as Golden Ball.'

'The Miss Armitage I saw was a tall, strapping girl with glorious eyes.'

'Diana Armitage,' said Mr Flanders, looking wise. 'Don't like men. Well-known fact in Berham county.'

There was another comfortable silence.

'Perhaps I might try my luck in that direction,' yawned Mr Emberton.

Mr Flanders raised his eyebrows so high that they nearly vanished into his hair. 'You, Jack, a marrying man!'

'I did not say anything about marriage.'

'Well, you can't go gathering the rosebuds of vicars' daughters.'

'I wasn't contemplating anything so sinful. I see a means whereby I might be able to pry some pocket money for myself out of the Armitage sons-in-law.'

'Don't tangle with them,' said Mr Flanders. 'It won't fadge. Murmurs and whispers among the ton that it's been tried before with no success. Powerful lot, the Armitage sons-in-law.'

'I am already much enamoured of the fair Diana. Just how I like them. Spicy.'

'Looks sulky to me. Vicar ain't going to encourage the advances of a card sharp, anyways.'

Jack Emberton half rose from his seat, his bulk menacing against the candlelight. 'I mean gentleman of fortune,' gabbled Mr Flanders.

'Exactly, my friend, and don't forget it. I have made a tidy bit at the tables of St James's and I have a mind to rusticate. So I shall look about for some small estate to rent, as near the vicarage as possible. You will put it about that I am a man of means, Jack Emberton, gentleman, recently returned to this country and desirous of finding a bride. Now, is there anything else about the family I should know? Any way to ingratiate myself with the good vicar? Donate something to the church?'

'Donate something to that precious hunt of his. Mr Armitage cares more for hounds than for souls. There's gossip about that Miss Diana rides like the wind.'

'An Amazon after mine own heart,' grinned Jack Emberton.

'I say, if you're going to get up to anything scandalous, don't drag me into it,' said Mr Flanders nervously.

'I mean, introducing you to the gentlemen with money to burn in St James's is one thing, helping you to blackmail is another.'

'Stop using that word,' said Mr Emberton harshly. 'You have benefited well from my gaming skills. Stick by me and you will profit—as you have profited before. We will set out in the morning to find me a suitable residence.'

By morning the wind had veered around to the north-east, a perfect day for hunting, with low ragged clouds dragging over the bare winter fields.

Diana sat miserably in her room, listening to the bustle below. She could not even bear to look out of the window.

Gradually, the sounds faded as the hunt moved off. A gnawing boredom beset her. The best hunting weather they had had this age and here she was, cribbed, cabined and confined, and all because she had the ill luck to be born a woman.

The squire would never have recognized her in man's hunting dress. She sat up suddenly. The squire would *not* recognize her. She would join the hunt. Her father would not dare betray her in front of everyone. He would rant and rave at her afterwards. But if he caught that old dog fox that had been plaguing him for so long she was sure he would forgive her anything.

She scrambled into her 'disguise', and then hesitated at the door of her bedroom. Usually on hunt days she made her escape before either Frederica or her mother was awake, hiding in the shadows of the stairs to make sure none of the servants was about. She whirled around and marched to the window, lifted the sash, climbed out and made her way nimbly down the ivy.

Her mare, Blarney, nuzzled her and pawed the ground, as anxious as Diana to be off with the hunt.

Diana judged they would start at Brook covert. And so she rode out, praying that the hunt would not prove to be miles away.

The vicar had been delayed reaching the covert by the worries of the squire. Squire Radford had confessed himself amazed to find little Frederica confined to the house. She was turning dreamy and strange, he said severely, and should be at a ladies' seminary, turning her mind to geography and the use of the globes instead of addling her brain with novels from the circulating library in Hopeminster. Fretting with impatience, the vicar ground out a promise to send Frederica back to school, although he saw no point in educating females. He had once thought it a good thing, but now he considered it a waste of time, since all the gentlemen seemed to prefer ladies with uninformed minds.

They were approaching the wild, straggling place that was Brook covert when, out of the corner of his eye, the vicar saw his daughter Diana come riding up. Was ever a man so plagued!

'Who is that young gentleman?' asked the squire, turning his head and narrowing his eyes before the wind.

'Friend of a friend,' muttered the vicar angrily. 'Pay no heed, Jimmy. We've work afoot.'

He dismounted, shouting, 'I feel in my bones the beast is in there.'

Sure enough, hounds were barely in when the old dog fox broke at the far end and went away like a greyhound. The vicar came tearing out to the 'holloa', red in the face, and blowing the 'gone-away' note for all he was worth.

Hounds were well away and going hard on the strong scent which comes with a north-east wind after a night of rain.

The vicar was riding an Irish mare that day, Turpin by Uncle Charlie out of Kettle. It was the mare's first hunt. All was well in the beginning, with Turpin flying over the flat ground. She took her first stone wall like a bird.

'Yee-up!' yelled the delighted vicar, waving his shovel hat. Behind him, on a great roan, came the little figure of the squire.

Diana drew alongside, completely absorbed in the chase. They reached the higher moorland which rose gently above Hope-worth and they could catch glimpses of the fox racing along while hounds swooped up and over the slopes like gulls. The chase led the hunt far afield that day as they raced by Harham, Badger Bank, Buckstead Park, over Berham moors, past Banting to Windham, circling round to the far side of Hope-minster. And still the old fox ran like the wind.

And then as black clouds built up to the west, as the light began to fail fast, the old fox simply disappeared. Hounds circled, baffled. It seemed impossible. It was not as if the fox had disappeared in brush and woodland. It had vanished in the middle of an open heath.

Diana realized she was absolutely exhausted. A drop of sleet whipped against her cheek. The wind gave a great roar. The Reverend Charles Armitage cursed and ranted and raved so much that the squire feared he would do himself an injury.

'Such language!' exclaimed the little squire. 'Our young friend over there will be shocked at such an exhibition.'

'Ah, our *young friend!*' hissed the vicar. Diana gave him one horrified look and galloped away as fast as her now tired and exhausted horse could carry her. More than anyone else did Diana know that her father was not quite sane on the hunting field.

The vicar glared after the flying figure of his daughter.

The squire edged his large horse close to that of the vicar. 'Tell me, Charles,' he said mildly. 'How long have you been allowing poor Diana to masquerade as a man?

Diana rode off into the increasing force of the storm. At last she stopped and turned around. There was no sign of her father. There was no sign of anything. Sleet, great blinding sheets of it, roared across the heaving blackness of the countryside.

Somehow, Diana knew the squire's sharp gaze had penetrated her disguise. For all his gentle ways, Squire Radford could influence her father as no other person could. Her hunting days were over.

She edged her horse slowly forward into the storm, not knowing where she was. Familiar landscapes were blotted out. It was imperative she should find warmth and shelter for her mare, Blarney. Her own comfort could wait.

And then, through the driving sleet, she thought she saw a flicker of light and headed in that direction.

CHAPTER TWO

It was like some fairy light. At one moment it looked near and the next it seemed to have danced a mile away. Diana had dismounted and was leading her horse when she all but collided with a pair of tall iron gates.

Sending up a prayer of thanks for her scarlet coat, that badge of the huntsman which easily enabled him to demand shelter for the night, Diana called out, 'Gate, ho! Gate, I say!' But only the wind howling in the branches above her head came as an answer. She tried the massive handle only to find that the gates were securely locked. She led her tired horse along the shelter of a high wall, looking for a way to get in. She had gone about a mile when she came to a part of the old mossy wall that had been broken. Taking the reins firmly in her hands she coaxed and patted Blarney, urging the mare over the pile of strewn boulders and into the dark blackness of a wooded estate. Praying that some roving gamekeeper would not take her for a poacher and shoot her, Diana stumbled through the woods until she arrived at a smooth stretch of long driveway.

There again was the light, clearly seen now at the end of the drive.

Soon she was able to pick out the bulk of a great house, a more solid black against the blackness of the night.

It was only when she was raising her hand to the knocker that she felt a qualm of unease. Her appearance as a man had never really been put to the test. Certainly several of the farmers had hunted with her father, but they only actually saw her on the hunting field. She had made a point of disappearing as soon as the hunt was over.

Blarney gave a soft whinny behind her.

Pulling her curly brimmed beaver down over her eyes, Diana seized the knocker and gave three vigorous raps.

There was a long silence broken only by the howling of the wind.

Then just as she was reaching her hand up to the knocker again, the door swung open, revealing a tall man in a dressing gown holding a candle in a brass stick.

For a long moment they surveyed each

other in silence. The gentleman's dressing gown was double breasted and made of dark blue quilted silk. A fine cambric shirt showed at his neck and ruffles of fine cambric lace at his wrists. He had hair that was so fair it was almost white, tied at the back of his neck with a black silk ribbon. He had wide spaced eyes, an odd green and gold colour. His nose was aristocratic with flaring nostrils and his mouth was long and thin and rather cruel. Diana found she had to look up at him, something she hardly ever had to do, most of the population of the county being as short as her father.

The gentleman's eyes took in the sodden scarlet of Diana's hunting coat and the mud of her breeches. He waited politely, and when Diana did not speak, he said, 'Lost your way, young huntsman?'

His voice was pleasant and mellow with a husky note in it, but a voice used to giving orders for all that.

Diana gulped and nodded.

'And you want stabling for your horse?'

Diana nodded again.

'You aren't dumb by any chance?'

Diana shook her head.

'I do not usually trouble my servants at

this hour since they are all very old but I will fetch Harry, one of the grooms.'

He turned about, leaving Diana standing on the step. Her host's idea of not troubling the servants seemed a complicated one. He rang the bell and the butler arrived, pulling on his coat. The butler was told to summon the page who was told to run round to the stables and fetch Harry.

But it was the sight of the butler that made Diana's heart somersault. She recognized the Osbadiston's butler, Chalmers, he who had replaced the much-loved black butler before old Osbadiston's death. This gentleman must be Lord Dantrey, although he was not at all young, thought Diana. Why, he must be all of thirty-five which was nearly middle-aged.

'I think I will accompany our young friend to the stables,' said Lord Dantrey when the groom arrived. The butler, Chalmers, produced a silk umbrella. Lord Dantrey languidly waved one white hand. The groom led the way, then Diana, and then Lord Dantrey, shielded from the rain by a tall footman holding the umbrella over his head, the footman having been summoned by the butler.

At first Diana was too concerned for the

welfare of her mare to think about the predicament she was in. First she gave the thirsty horse half a bucket of tepid water, for to give it a large bucket of cold water might bring it out in a sweat. She thoroughly checked its coat for the presence of small wounds or thorns. Then she rubbed the horse down and covered it with a blanket warmed at the tack room fire. At last she was finished and was able to turn and reluctantly face her host.

'I know this is the old Osbadiston house,' said Diana gruffly. 'I have been here many times as a child. You must be Lord Dantrey.'

Lord Dantrey was sitting at his ease beside the tack room fire.

'You have the advantage of me,' he said. 'Your name, young man?'

'David,' said Diana, blushing furiously. 'David Armitage. I am a nephew of the Reverend Charles Armitage of Hopeworth.'

'Ah, yes, the vicar with the six beautiful daughters. Are they all married?'

'The four eldest, I believe, sir.'

'Which leaves?'

'Diana and Frederica, my lord.'

'And are the remaining two as beautiful

as the other four?"

'Well enough in their way,' mumbled Diana.

'You disappoint me. I would have supposed them to be diamonds of the first water. I had hoped to meet the divine Armitages quite soon. I am recovering from an illness and have not been about much.'

Diana looked down at her muddy boots. She desperately wanted to escape. There is nothing more terrifying to the immature country dweller than an exquisite, languid sophisticate, and Lord Dantrey somehow contrived to make even cleanliness seem decadent. His shirt frill was *too* white, his nails too immaculately manicured, and the sheen on his white hair was like frost on flax.

Lord Dantrey rose to his feet. 'We can't stay here all night. Come along, Mr Armitage, and I will find you some supper.'

'I am putting you to a lot of trouble,' said Diana desperately. 'If you would be so good as to allow me to leave my horse here until morning, I will return this night to Hopeworth . . .'

'You can't go out in this storm,' said Lord Dantrey gently. 'What would the good vicar say? Also, I have been too much in mine own company of late. We shall talk.'

Diana groaned inwardly but had not the courage to protest further.

As Lord Dantrey led the way back to the house and then ushered Diana into a comfortable library, she regained a little courage.

'I cannot sit down in my dirt, my lord,' she protested.

'Neither you can,' smiled Lord Dantrey. 'My housekeeper will take you up to the room that has been prepared for you and my valet will attend to you.'

Feeling she had roused the whole household, Diana followed a stately-looking housekeeper up a wide, carved oak staircase. When the valet had found her a pair of breeches, a shirt and a dressing gown, Diana told him that she preferred to dress herself and locked the door firmly behind the little valet. She was not afraid that any of the servants might recognize her. None of them had seen her since she was very young.

The breeches and shirt were rather long. The dressing gown was fortunately a bulky, padded affair which successfully hid her female figure. Once dressed, she rang for the valet and told him that her soiled hunting clothes were to be left in her room and *not* taken down to the kitchens for cleaning.

Diana planned to make her escape during the night.

'Very good, sir,' said the valet, trying not to stare at this odd gentleman who apparently meant to dine with Lord Dantrey, still wearing a muddy beaver hat.

'Tell my lord I will be with him in a very short while,' said Diana. Once again, she locked the door. She pulled off her hat and looked in despair at the masses of black hair cascading about her shoulders.

There was only one thing to be done. She picked up a long sharp pair of scissors and began to cut her hair, feeling oddly weak and feminine and tearful when she finally picked up the shorn tresses and threw them on the fire.

Her hair had a natural curl which disguised the amateur cut.

Despite her fear, Diana still managed to notice the richness of the furnishings on her way back downstairs. On the first floor a gallery ran around three sides where one could look down into the spacious hall. Diana remembered how it had looked in the

days of the waning Osbadiston fortunes . . .
cold and shabby. Now the hall was carpeted,
the walls hung with fine paintings, and set
about with sculpture. Candles had been lit,
many candles, an overwhelming expense to
welcome one tired provincial huntsman.

'If only I were a man,' thought Diana for
about the thousandth time in her young life.
'I would be nervous, but we could talk and
eat, and then I could retire to bed with an
easy conscience. Can he possibly guess I am
a woman? Oh, I am so tired and I must be
on my guard.'

When she walked into the library she
noticed with a feeling of thankfulness that it
was not brightly lit. A table had been set
with cold meat, bread and wine. Diana's
stomach gave an unladylike rumble, remind-
ing her that she had not eaten all day.

Lord Dantrey waved her into a chair at the
table and sat down opposite her. He carved
her some roast beef and poured her a glass of
wine, and, as she bent her head, he studied
her cropped hair with interest.

'Where do you live when you are not at
the vicarage?' he asked abruptly. Diana
choked on a mouthful of wine and murmured an apology. 'I live at Datchwood on

the other side of Berham county.'

'How old are you, Mr Armitage, if it is not too personal a question?'

'Nineteen, my lord.'

'Indeed! I would have thought you younger despite your inches. What awaits you in the future?'

'I do not know, my lord.'

'You have dreams and ambitions, surely?'

Diana gave a little sigh. What did one more lie matter?

She thought of the many hours she had daydreamed of having the freedom of a man.

'I should like, above all things,' she said slowly, 'to have the freedom to wander about London and discover its wonders for myself without being tied to the environs of St James's Square. I would like,' she continued dreamily, beginning to feel the heady effects of the wine, 'to be a Dandy.'

'Not a very creditable ambition,' said Lord Dantrey.

'But surely a Dandy is the admiration of society?'

'Not he. Do you know how a Dandy is described? A coxcomb, a fop, an empty-headed vain person. The Dandy was got by Vanity out of Affection—his dam, Petit

Maître or Maccaroni—his grand-dam, Fribble—his great grand-dam, Bronze—his great-great-great grand-dam, Coxcomb—and his earliest ancestor, Fop. His uncle, Impudence—his three brothers, Trick, Humbug and Fudge, and allied to the extensive family of Shuffletons.'

'Oh, dear. Then I shall be a Buck, a Blood, a Choice Spirit.'

'Worse and worse,' mocked Lord Dantrey. 'All the same and all quite terrible. A riotous set of disorderly young men who imagine that their noise, bluster, warwhoops and impertinence impress those who come into contact with them with the opinion that they are men of spirit and fashion. The nocturnal exploits of the true, high-mettled and fast-going Blood consist of throwing a waiter out of a tavern window; pinking a sedan chairman or jarvey who is so uncivil as to demand his fare; milling and boxing up the Charlies; kicking up rows at Ranelagh or Vauxhall; driving stage coaches; getting up prize fights; breaking shop windows with penny pieces thrown from a Hackney coach; bilking a turnpike man and at other times painting out his list of tolls payable. What else? Funking a cobbler—that is, blowing smoke into his stall; smoking cigars at divans and club houses; fleecing each other in the Hells around Jermyn Street; drinking champagne at Charlie Wright's in the Haymarket, claret and brandy at Offley's in Covent Garden, and early pearls and dognose at the Coal Hole; wearing large whiskers and false noses and moustaches; exchanging blackguard badinage with women of the town in and about Covent Garden, the Haymarket and Piccadilly, shouting, "Demme, that's yer sort. Keep it up! Keep it up!" '

Lord Dantrey leaned back in his chair and watched with interest the tide of red rising in Diana's cheeks.

'Forgive my use of cant,' said Lord Dantrey. 'I had supposed a young man like yourself would have heard worse on the hunting field.'

Diana affected a yawn and leaned back in her chair, thrusting her hands in her breeches pockets. 'I was not turning red with embarrassment,' she said. 'The heat from the fire is great and I confess to being deuced tired.'

'Then finish your wine and go to bed.' He watched her intently while she picked up her glass. 'I have been away from England for a very long time,' he said, 'and I have a mind to savour the delights of town once more. If you wish, you may tell your father I will take you as my guest.'

'You are too kind, my lord,' gulped Diana. 'Unfortunately, m-my f-father is d-dead and I am the sole companion of my widowed mother.'

'Sad. But should you change your mind, my offer still stands. And now to bed. Can you find your way?'

'Oh, yes,' gabbled Diana, springing to her feet and oversetting a chair. Miserably, she quickly bent and picked it up. 'I thank you for your hospitality, my lord, and bid you goodnight.'

'Good night, Mr Armitage,' said Lord Dantrey softly. 'Sleep well.'

Those green and gold eyes of his held a mocking look.

Diana ran up the stairs to her room, locking the door behind her and letting out a deep breath only when she was sure she was safe.

Safe? What an odd thought. For her host had been all that was proper.

Diana went to the window and leaned out. The storm had died away and the night was cold and still. She pulled a chair up to the window after changing back into her riding clothes and settled down until she judged the time right to make her escape. She would leave a letter for Lord Dantrey, of course, and then hope and pray she would never see him again.

But as she sat waiting, his offer to take her to London returned to plague her. If only, before the rigours of feminine boredom closed down on her for life, she could be free just once.

She had not been missed. Frederica had gone to sleep over a book, Mrs Armitage had dosed herself with laudanum, and the vicar had spent a tiring and humiliating evening with Squire Radford.

The vicar could never stand up to the normally gentle squire and sometimes thought bitterly that Jimmy Radford had been sent to earth for the sole purpose of giving uncomfortable jabs to Charles Armitage's conscience.

But the matter, put by the squire, had alarmed the vicar. He, the vicar, had put his daughter's future in jeopardy. It would get about that she had been hunting, dressed as a man, and riding astride. Her morals, her manners, and the intactness of her virginity would be in question. Her value on the marriage market would slump.

No man would wish to be allied to a girl who had shown herself capable of the grossest, the most indecent behaviour. Diana must be *broken*, like a wild colt, the squire had insisted. The bit must be put in her mouth and the saddle on her back before some man took up the reins. Diana, in short, must be *feminized*. There was time and enough for little Frederica. Schooling and the company of her peers was what she needed at present. It would be arranged that she would be sent to a boarding school for young ladies. The squire privately thought Mrs Armitage a useless sort of mother. As for Diana? She must be sent to Lady Godolphin in Hanover Square as soon as possible to begin her training for her debut at the next Season. Lady Godolphin had been instrumental in bringing out the elder girls. Let her do what she could with Diana.

As a weak protest the vicar pointed out that a certain Lord Dantrey had taken the Osbadiston place and was reported to be rich. That hope was quickly dashed. Mark

Dantrey, the squire had said severely, was in his mid-thirties, and although he had been travelling abroad for some years, he had had the reputation of being a terrible rake when he was younger. Not at all the sort of son-in-law for the Armitage stable.

Weary with worry, bad conscience, and the aches and pains of a long day's hunting, the vicar retired to bed, vowing to face Diana in the morning.

Diana had arrived home in the small hours, having climbed back up the ivy to her room, after stabling her still-weary horse. She took off her hunting clothes and locked them carefully away in a trunk so that the maid, Sarah, would not find them. Something would have to be done about her hair before she faced her father in the morning. He would be in a towering rage in any case and Diana did not want to make his temper any the worse.

She had managed to make her escape from Lord Dantrey's mansion without even alerting one of the servants. She had left a letter of thanks, apologizing for her early departure. Before she fell asleep, she heard Lord Dantrey's voice in her ears offering to take her to London.

Sarah, the maid, who had been rattling at Diana's locked bedroom door for most of the morning, succeeded at last in awakening her. She exclaimed in amazement over Diana's cropped hair, wondering aloud why miss should take it upon her head to change her hairstyle in the middle of the night. Sarah finally decided that with a little extra curling she could contrive a style she had recently seen in one of Mrs Armitage's magazines— 'irregular curls, confined in the Eastern style and blended with flowers.' Sarah, for all her brash country air, was a good lady's maid with a sophisticated touch that Betty had lacked.

'Flowers are a bit odd for morning, Miss Diana,' she said, neatly placing small pink silk rosebuds among Diana's black curls, 'but master'll be pleased to see you looking so pretty.'

Diana consented to wear a Polonese robe with a petticoat of fine cambric and jaconet muslin.

When she went downstairs the vicar was waiting for her, striding up and down, slapping his short riding whip against his boot.

He swung around furiously as Diana entered the room but his angry stare softened somewhat as he beheld the unusually elegant Diana Armitage.

'Sit down,' he barked, 'and listen to me. Squire Radford recognized you and so there's no more hunting for you, miss. Before any more damage is done, I'm sending you to Lady Godolphin to get some training in the genteel arts. Your manners is awful to behold,' said the vicar, pausing to spit in the fire. 'Thought there might be hopes in the direction of Lord Dantrey but it seems he's some old rake and Ann Carter is welcome to him.'

Although Diana had expected hunting to be banned, she had not expected to feel such pain and such loss. 'There are things a gently-bred miss does not do,' went on her father inexorably, 'and hunting's one of them. I've allowed you too much licence and it's time to mend your ways.'

'I don't want to get married,' said Diana. 'Ever.'

'Stuff. A strong man is just what you need and Lady Godolphin will see to it that you get one.'

'If she is not too involved in her own

amours,' said Diana caustically.

'Enough o' that, miss. We all know she ain't exactly a saint but Minerva tells me she's settled down amazing.'

'Can't I go to Minerva?' begged Diana, her eyes filling with tears. Before her marriage, Minerva, the eldest, had acted as 'mother' to the smaller girls, and although they had all chafed somewhat under her strict rule, that rule had brought them love and warmth and security.

'Minerva's baby is ailing, not Julian, Charles. Annabelle ain't got children but she's so taken up with that husband o' hers, she won't have time to give you her undivided attention and Daphne and Deirdre are in the country. You'll be best off with Lady Godolphin.'

'Now I've got this here letter to say you will be arriving on Wednesday of next week. We won't trouble to wait for a reply,' added the vicar with a crafty look. 'Just you give this to the post boy when he comes.'

The vicar rode over to the hall that afternoon to pay a visit on his brother, Sir Edwin Armitage. If there was any bad gossip going about the neighborhood about Diana then Sir Edwin would be sure to know. Sir Edwin had never been able to understand why the poor vicarage girls had married so well while his own daughters, Emily and Josephine, had fared so badly.

Josephine was now married to a middle-aged squire over in Hopeminster, and Emily had grown plain and sour and like to be an ape leader. The only time she showed signs of animation was when a letter arrived from America from Mr Wentwater, the former slave trader who had plagued the vicar's family. No one had heard of his aunt, Lady Wentwater, for some time, and her ivy-covered mansion still stood empty.

As usual, Sir Edwin, thin, pompous and fussily dressed, quite obviously did not relish a visit from his brother. He loathed the vicar's hunt, which he blamed for the ruin of his crops and the scarcity of his pheasants.

But although Sir Edwin made a few snide remarks about Frederica's bookishness and Diana's hoydenish ways, he showed no sign of having heard anything of Diana's hunting exploits. The vicar then rode over to the squire's to tell Jimmy Radford of Diana's forthcoming visit to London, waxing quite eloquent and sanctimonious over the whole business as if he had thought of it him-self.

Diana spent most of the day in a daze of misery. She dared not go near the kennels or stables for fear of breaking down. It was only when she was sitting in her room in the early evening that she suddenly realized the sound of sobbing was coming from *outside* of her and not inside. Frederica! Diana went quickly along to her sister's room.

Frederica was lying face down on the bed, crying her eyes out. Diana gathered the younger girl's slender body into her arms and rocked her against her breast.

'There, there, Freddie,' said Diana. 'Tell me about it. You are always such a dreamy little thing, I never thought you were so unhappy.'

It was some time before Frederica could compose herself enough to reply. She raised a blotched and tearstained face to Diana's. 'I am being sent away,' she moaned. 'I am to go to school to *board*. I-I d-don't want to go away. I'm *frightened*.' Frederica began to cry again.

'Shhh!' said Diana. 'Remember how fright-ened the boys were when they finally set out for Eton? And Minerva told me *she* was frightened when she had to leave for London.'

'Minerva!' exclaimed Frederica, sitting up and beginning to dry her eyes. 'I would not have thought Merva afraid of *anything.*'

'We are all afraid of something, sometime,' sighed Diana. 'I am to go away, too, Freddie. Did you know I had been hunting with papa?'

'Oh, yes,' said Frederica. 'I thought it odd, but I did not tell anyone, not even Mama.'

'I went out with the hunt yesterday,' said Diana, 'and Squire Radford recognized me and read Papa a sermon. So I am to go to Lady Godolphin to be taught the arts of a lady. Pah!'

'Lady Godolphin!' Frederica gave a watery smile. 'I have never noticed Lady Godolphin quite behaving like a lady. I love her dearly, but she is so very shocking and gets all her words mixed up and she wears such a lot of paint.'

'Papa feels she is a lucky chaperone because of the good marriages of Minerva, Annabelle, Daphne and Deirdre—although it is my opinion Lady Godolphin had not much to do with any of their marriages. The fact is that all the four are so very beautiful they could have married *anyone*, with or without Lady Godolphin's help.'

Frederica took Diana's hand in her own and gave it a squeeze. 'I think you are more beautiful than any of us when you are not trying to be a man, Diana. I like your new coiffure. Vastly fetching. Don't you want to fall in love?'

'Not I,' said Diana. 'All I want is freedom.' Her large eyes glittered with tears of frustration as she thought of all the beautiful hunting days ahead, days in which she would be trapped and confined in some stuffy saloon. 'And yet there might be some man for me, Freddie. There was this gypsy woman on the Hopeminster Road who said a tall and dark man was going to enter my life.'

'Pooh, they always say that,' said Frederica.

'How would *you* know,' scoffed Diana. 'You haven't even met a gypsy.'

'But in the books I read, gypsies are always saying things like that. Of course, it comes true in books . . .'

'There you are, then!'

'Never mind the gypsies. Do you think the other girls at the school will be cruel to me?'

'Nobody could be cruel to you, Freddie. You'll have friends to talk to and lots of books to read. It is very lonely here. I wish I were a man. I wish I could run away. Look here, I'll tell you a secret, Freddie, only you're not to breathe a word to anyone, not even if they threaten you with terrible things.'

Frederica sat up in bed and hugged her knees with excitement.

'Do tell, Diana. I won't breathe a word to a soul.'

'Well, it was yesterday. Last night, as a matter of fact. I had been out hunting, but Squire Radford was there. Papa failed to catch that old dog fox that's been plaguing him and he was mad with rage. You know what he can be like, Freddie! So I simply rode away. But the storm came down and it was so dreadful and so black that I did not know where I was. And then, all at once, I saw a light through the blackness and headed towards it . . .'

Frederica listened enthralled to the tale of Diana and Lord Dantrey. When Diana had finished, Frederica said, 'I heard Papa tell Mama that cards are not to be sent to this Lord Dantrey on account of his being so wicked. Mama said . . .'

'You mean Mama is alive to the world again?'

'Yes, she was actually in the parlour for quite two hours. You know how she *can* be sometimes.'

Both sister smiled at each other in sympathetic understanding. They had become so used to their mother's increasingly long bouts of self-inflicted illness from trying out this or that new patent medicine that they still found it rather a shock when she appeared back downstairs, for however brief a period, with all her wits about her.

'Anyway,' went on Frederica. 'Papa was telling her about meeting a Mrs Carter and her daughter, Ann, at the Chumleys. He said this Ann was very beautiful and that Mrs Carter was trying to catch Lord Dantrey for her. Mama shook her head and said she had heard of this Lord Dantrey some time ago. He ran away with a lady and *ruined* her.'

'Perhaps he was very young,' said Diana, wondering at the same time why she should wish to leap to Lord Dantrey's defence.

'I have heard that gentlemen often do odd things when they are young. He was most correct in *my* presence though a trifle broad in his speech, which was understandable considering he thought me to be a man. Oh, I did not tell you! He asked me about my ambitions and I told him I had always wanted to have the freedom to wander about London without being confined to the social life of the West End. He said he would take me to London should I wish to go.'

'That was very wrong of him and very shocking.'

'Not shocking at all, you little goose. He thought me a man.'

'Do you think he will recognize you if he ever sees you as you are now?'

'I should not think so,' said Diana slowly. 'He would merely think there was a strong family resemblance. I am relieved he is not considered socially acceptable. For if he did visit us here he would be bound to ask after David Armitage and he would find out such a person did not exist. He might even be asked to describe this David Armitage, and if he talked about a young huntsman then Papa would most certainly guess that David Armitage was me. I would be ruined. Oh, dear. I never thought of that. It teases my mind now, Freddie, that offer of his. I would not be in any danger from him since he thinks me a man. It would be such fun to wander the streets of London, free as a bird.'

'Lady Godolphin would have the Runners out looking for you. When you did not arrive, she would send an express to Papa.'

'I forgot to give the letter to the post boy,' said Diana. 'I have been so miserable. Would it not be wonderful if I were to go to London for a week as a man? And then after that one week of blessed freedom I would be more in the frame of mind to suffer the rigours of polite society.'

'But you would not do such a thing, of course!' said Frederica, round-eyed.

'I can dream, can't I?' smiled Diana. 'Come, Freddie, admit I have cheered you with my nonsense. You will go to your school and I to my social training. You are only to spend a year, you know. Because by that time you will be thinking of your own come-out. I might even marry, and I'll send for you and you can live with me and addle your head with novels all day long.'

'Oh, Diana,' cried Frederica, throwing her arms about her sister. 'I should like that of all things. I will be good and go to school. And you must promise to write to me as much as you can.'

'Of course I shall.' Diana put her arms about her sister again, talking soothing nonsense, her voice soft and comforting, while the light faded and a mournful wind sighed in the eaves.

After a little while, Frederica, exhausted from her crying, fell asleep, her head against Diana's breast.

Diana sat holding her, occasionally stroking her hair, staring into the darkness of the room. She would let Frederica sleep for a little before awakening her and helping her to prepare for bed.

Then Diana thought of the letter waiting in her room, the letter to Lady Godolphin. Now, just suppose she, Diana, kept that letter. Just suppose she packed a bag with some of the twins' spare clothes. Peregrine and James had grown so tall that she could easily fit their clothes. And just suppose she asked Lord Dantrey to take her to London . . .

She would have to leave the vicarage with Sarah and John Summers, the coachman, with all her trunks corded and ready for London.

But Mrs Armitage was very dependent on

young Sarah to minister to her ailments. If she could persuade her father that Sarah should return immediately with the coach . . .

If somehow she could leave her trunks, with all her female clothes, at Lady Godolphin's *without* Lady Godolphin seeing her . . . If she could take a bag with the boys' clothes and escape for a week . . . Perhaps she could alter the date of that letter to say she was arriving the following Wednesday . . .

And so Diana's thoughts ran on and on, still not realizing she was not day-dreaming, and that she had actually made up her mind to try to accept Lord Dantrey's invitation.

CHAPTER THREE

The letter to Lady Godolphin lay hidden with Diana's hunting clothes as the day for her departure to London approached. The news that two young men had taken up residence in Lady Wentwater's mansion gave the vicar slight pause. Perhaps a suitable husband might be found for Diana close by without incurring the horrendous expense of a Season. One of the young men, a Mr Jack Emberton, was reported to be an Adonis although his friend, Mr Peter Flanders, was judged only passable. But, on reflection, the vicar decided he would always be suspicious of anyone staying at Lady Wentwater's, albeit a pair of innocent lessees. The fact that this Mr Emberton was reported to be tall and dark made Diana wonder briefly if he might be the man the gypsy woman had seen in her future, but she was too busy with plans and schemes to give it very much thought.

The coach was to deposit her at Lady Godolphin's and return immediately with Sarah and John Summer. So far, so good.

Diana at last decided to trust to the gods and try to arrange to arrive in London at an hour when Lady Godolphin was still abed—in fact, any time before two in the afternoon. The Godolphin servants had not seen her since she was much younger. Mice, the butler, was short-sighted. The footmen were new to the household. If she could send the coach away *before* the door was answered, she could pretend to be her own lady's maid and say she had come to leave Miss Diana's trunks and that Miss Diana would be arriving the following week. Then, provided that bit of the plan worked, what to do?

She would have to find some quiet hostelry where she could change into her man's disguise. Before she left, she must write to Lord Dantrey and say she would be staying at . . . where? Limmer's in Conduit Street. That was it. Papa had said all the gentlemen stayed there.

And then, all at once, when it was but two days until her departure, Diana decided the whole thing was madness. A tearful Frederica had been sent off to school.

Frederica, believing Diana's plans to be merely an amusement, had, nonetheless, encouraged Diana in her fantasies. Now, with Frederica gone, Diana felt weak and helpless.

That lasted until the day before she was to leave, the day the vicar rode out hunting. The morning was windy and fine. Diana clutched the windowsill and stared down at the prancing horses, at the sunlight gleaming on the sleek coats of the hounds and felt a lump rise in her throat. It was not *fair*. She was the only Armitage who shared her father's love of the hunt. Once Peregrine and James had been allowed to go out hunting, they had immediately lost all interest in the sport. She should have been born a boy. Angry tears filled Diana's eyes and blurred the scene below.

She, Diana, deserved just one little bit of freedom. She did not give a fig for Lord Dantrey's wicked reputation. She remembered how nervous she had felt in his company, but put that nervousness down to fear of discovery. He had been easy to converse with. She was in absolutely no danger so long as he believed her a man, and there was no reason why he should think otherwise. Squire Radford had only found her out because he had known her all his life.

Diana sat down at the pretty little escritoire in her room, pulled forward a piece of paper, and began to write to Lord Dantrey.

There was a heart-stopping moment before she climbed in the carriage two days later when Diana felt all her plans were about to be ruined. For Mrs Armitage was audibly wondering whether she ought to accompany her daughter. She fretted to see dear Minerva and the grandchildren, which Diana cynically translated into pining for the apothecary shops of London.

To Diana's immeasurable relief, Mrs Armitage, with that irritatingly drooping manner of hers which sat so ill on the round, plump features of a greying lady, decided not to go. Diana embraced her warmly, saying firmly she would send Sarah back *immediately*. Diana threw Sarah a warning look, and the maid, who had hoped for at least an hour to look at the London shops, pettishly tossed her head.

Mr Pettifor, the vicar's overworked curate,

sidled up in his usual apologetic way to say his goodbyes and give Miss Diana his blessing, a task which the vicar should have performed had the vicar not been out hunting again.

At last the coach moved off and Diana leaned back with a sigh of relief.

Nothing could stop her now from making her bid for freedom!

As the coach neared Lady Wentwater's old place a horseman rode straight out into the road, causing John Summer to swear and rein in his horses. The horseman swung around by the side of the carriage and could be heard apologizing to the enraged John. Diana let down the glass and looked out.

Here he was at last! The man the gypsy had talked about. He was tall and well-built with broad shoulders and an excellent seat. He swept off his hat at the sight of Diana and made a bow. His hair was thick and black and his eyes a merry twinkling blue.

'My deepest apologies, ma'am,' he said. 'Have I the honour of addressing the beautiful Diana Armitage?'

'I am Miss Armitage, sir, and you are . . . ?'

'Emberton, Miss Diana. Jack Emberton at

your service. Never tell me you are leaving Hopeworth just when I have found you?'

Diana, who felt she ought to depress the warmth of his compliments, found she somehow could not. Mr Emberton had a delightful smile which was reflected in his eyes.

'I am leaving to stay with a relative, sir.'

'And may I beg your direction, Miss Diana, my divine angel?'

Diana felt this was going too far and even the bold Sarah gave her mistress's wrist a warning pinch.

'You are detaining us,' said Diana. 'Good day to you, Mr Emberton.'

She jerked up the window and the carriage moved on. But Diana felt filled with elation and excitement. The gypsy woman had not told a fairy tale. Jack Emberton was everything that Diana felt a man should be. She wished now she had not been so abrupt. And she was leaving Hopeworth just at this interesting point in time! Diana consoled herself with the thought that the gypsy would not have mentioned him entering her life if nothing was to come of it. Mr Emberton would no doubt call at the vicarage and would soon find her direction in town.

They put up for the night at a comfortable posting house much frequented by members of the Armitage family. Sarah moved into the attack as she was preparing Diana for bed. Would not miss *please* let poor Sarah just look at the shops for a little? Steeling herself, Diana refused, almost rudely, which sent the flighty maid into sulks for the rest of the journey on the following day.

Sarah was so angry with Diana that she was perfectly prepared to abandon her on Lady Godolphin's doorstep but John Summer was horrified at the very idea. What if her ladyship was gone from home? Vicar would never forgive him.

The odd-man who had been transformed into footman for the journey, complete with a pair of Minerva's old white silk stockings and one of the vicar's old wigs, helped John carry the trunks up the steps. Diana stole a look at the fob watch pinned to the bosom of her pelisse. Eleven-thirty in the morning. Hope and pray that Lady Godolphin was still abed! John performed a vigorous tattoo on the knocker, and, after a moment, Mice, Lady Godolphin's butler, opened the door.

'Thank you, John,' said Diana quickly. 'Mrs Armitage is anxious to see Sarah as soon as possible. Would you be so good, sir,' she said to Mice, dropping her voice on the 'sir' so that John would not hear what she said, 'as to help me with Miss Diana Armitage's trunks?'

Mice summoned two footmen. The trunks were loaded into the hall.

'Thank you, John,' said Diana sweetly and closed the door firmly on the startled coachman's face.

'Well, I dunno if I've ever had such hoity-toity treatment from one of the girls,' grumbled John as he swung himself up onto the box. 'No, not even from Miss Annabelle at her worst.'

Inside the hall, Diana, adopting a country burr, curtseyed to Mice. 'I'll be on my way, sir. I'm leavin' all 'cept that liddle box which is mine.'

'Why didn't you return to Hopeworth with the coach?' demanded Mice awfully.

'I have permission for to visit my mum what lives in the City, sir.'

'Very well, miss. Be on your way. Does Miss Diana Armitage arrive today? We was not informed.'

'In another week, sir. Could someone please find me a hack?'

Diana's request went down the servants' ranks, since no upper servant was going to stoop to run errands for any other servant, until the job was given to the page.

At last, seated in a smelly hack, Diana told the jehu to take her to the City to 'one of the coaching inns'. Then she searched in her reticule to make sure she had brought her money with her. Diana had had hopes of buying a new hunter and had saved every penny of the generous presents of money sent to her by her now wealthy elder sisters. She had now what seemed to her an immense fortune—one hundred pounds.

She was put down at the White Hart, near the street of the Lombards. Diana had enough sense to know that a reputable coaching inn would be one of the few places where a young lady travelling on her own would not cause curiosity or comment.

The inn was an old Tudor one with galleries running around a courtyard. After she had reserved a room and eaten a little cold beef and salad, she ventured out into the teeming streets of the City. But the richness of her clothes and the fact that she was unaccompanied by a maid caused heads to turn and stare. Because of his short-sightedness, Mice had not noticed her clothing, and, when the butler seemed to treat her as the servant she pretended to be, then the rest of Lady Godolphin's servants followed suit. Finally, when a party of apprentices began to pester her, she decided to return to her room and begin the masquerade. She had told Lord Dantrey she would be at Limmer's the following day, but all at once she wanted to get there that very evening.

She took great pains over her appearance. She had selected a blue swallowtail coat belonging to her brother, Peregrine, and leather breeches and a striped Marseillaise waistcoat belonging to his twin, James. She tried to tie her starched cravat into one of the fashionable styles she had seen but it seemed to have a life of its own, and at last she moulded it into a satisfactory shape by pleating down the starched cloth with her fingers. Then she teased and backcombed her short hair into a semblance of the Windswept and, with a carefully adopted swagger, sauntered downstairs to pay 'm'sister's shot, her having left sudden.'

Diana then returned to her room to collect her small trunk, satisfied that no one had taken her for a girl. Fortunately the pouter pigeon effect among the Dandies was in fashion. It was quite the tippy to walk with your buckrammed chest thrust forward and your bottom stuck out in the opposite direction, so Diana's well-padded chest —padded under the breasts, that is, to disguise their shape—did not look odd in the slightest.

She found a hack to take her to Limmer's. It was only when the ancient carriage rumbled up Holborn that Diana began to wonder if she had run mad. What if Lord Dantrey did not come? Could she possibly manage on her own?

Of course she could, she told herself firmly. Only look how well she had succeeded so far.

Limmer's was not at all what she expected. In the first place it was crowded, and several bloods were complaining loudly that they could not get rooms. In the second, it only took one glance to tell Diana that the hotel was extremely dirty.

When it came her turn, an experienced eye flicked from the youth of her face to the shabby trunk at her feet, and she was told, 'No, young sir. Nothing for another couple of weeks.'

'But you *must* have a room,' said Diana, made bold by desperation. For how on earth would Lord Dantrey find her if she had to move somewhere else?

'I am afraid not,' said the liveried clerk contemptuously. 'Not even the Duke of Devonshire could get in here this night.'

'I was to meet my friend, Lord Dantrey,' said Diana, keeping her voice as low and masculine as possible despite her distress. 'I must find some other accommodation and beg you to tell him my direction as soon as he arrives.'

The clerk's face suddenly performed a ludicrous change from hauteur to obsequiousness. 'Well, well,' he said, opening up a much fingerprinted ledger, 'we have not had the pleasure of his lordship's custom for many years. Is his lordship indeed back in this country from foreign parts?'

Diana nodded dumbly.

'I recall now that we have just had two cancellations. How it slipped my mind I cannot think. The George, sir,' he said, handing the grateful and amazed Diana a large key. 'Second floor. Charles, Mr . . . ?'

'Armitage. '

'Take Mr Armitage's box up to the George. Will you be dining here tonight, sir?'

Diana nodded.

She followed the porter up the stairs and into a grimy room furnished with an old four poster bed with dirty hangings and doubtful linen. A small seacoal fire smoked on the hearth.

After she had unpacked her very small stock of clothes culled from the twins' wardrobe, she made her way downstairs. She paused in the doorway of the dining room, her heart beating hard. There had obviously been a meeting of the Driving Club that day, rivals to the Four in Hand. The room was full of boozy bucks dressed in the same uniform; drab coloured coat with full skirts reaching to the heels, with three tiers of pockets and mother-of-pearl buttons, each the size of a crown piece, waistcoat with stripes of blue and yellow an inch wide, breeches of yellow plush with sixteen strings and a rosette at each knee, buff topped boots wrinkled down to the ankles, a bell-shaped white beaver hat, three and a half inches deep in the crown and the same width in the brim, and the whole ensemble decorated with a huge nosegay thrust into the buttonhole. To Diana, they all looked simply terrifying. She did not even know the company boasted three of the most admired Corinthians in London: Tom Akers, wearing a white beaver turned up with green, and with his front teeth filed so that he could spit like a coachman: Sir John Lade, who could drive the two off wheels of his phaeton over a sixpence at the start of a hundred yards: and Golden Ball Hughes, that most languid of sportsmen, doing his best to run through forty thousand pounds a year. Hard, rather truculent stares turned in her direction and the conversation died away.

Diana gave a nervous gulp and turned and fled upstairs, back to her room. She sat crouched beside the fire. She could never go through with it. All at once, a picture of Ann Carter rose before her mind's eye; pretty, dainty Ann. What if Mr Emberton fell in love with Ann? How silly she, Diana, had been to simply drive on. How missish and idiotish to believe in a dirty old gypsy. There was a knock at the door, but Diana stayed where she was, too frightened to answer it.

The door handle turned and the door swung open.

Lord Mark Dantrey stood on the threshold.

He was wearing a many-caped driving coat and a curly-brimmed beaver. He looked much taller and more elegant than Diana had remembered. He removed his hat, revealing that the old-fashioned length of his hair had been cut and styled into miraculous disorder, making poor Diana feel that her own attempts at the Windswept had been feeble, to say the least.

'I came early,' he said, coming into the room. 'Have you dined?'

Diana shook her head. 'I am not accustomed to town,' she said. 'Everyone seemed so drunk and noisy, and it is so very dirty here. Not at all what I expected.'

'Ah, well, that is Limmer's for you. It is so expensive that everyone swears they charge extra for the dirt. However their gin punch is very good and the meals are tolerable. Do you care to join me for supper?'

He saw the hesitation in Diana's face and added gently, 'There is a coffee house near here which will be much quieter, if you would prefer it.'

'Oh, yes,' said Diana gratefully. She went to the mirror to straighten her cravat and caught herself just in time as she was about to give a feminine pat to her curls.

What a difference it was to saunter along the London streets with such a tall and elegant companion. Diana gazed about her eagerly, mimicking the swaggering walk of the Bloods. They turned in at Hubbold's Coffee House and took seats in a high-backed booth. Diana began to relax. She had thought coffee houses would be noisy, boisterous places like the dining room at Limmer's, but this was more what she would imagine a gentleman's club to be. Everything was hushed and silent. Craning her head around the high back of the settle, she noticed men sitting quietly, writing, or reading newspapers.

Lord Dantrey ordered roast beef and salad and a bottle of hock. Diana would dearly have liked something else, but she was too frightened to say so. It seemed that Lord Dantrey considered burgundy and claret fit only for the ladies.

'I do not know any of this, sir,' said Diana. 'I fear I lack town bronze.'

'Innocence and a good heart are worth more than town bronze,' said Lord Dantrey. 'But it amuses me to take you about. Perhaps my last bachelor outing before I settle down to find myself a wife. Will you marry, think you, Mr Armitage?'

'Not I,' said Diana quickly. 'I have no time for the ladies.'

'Indeed! I thought youth was always romantic.'

'Perhaps. I am not without feeling for romance. I admire Lord Byron. *He* must be all that is romantic.'

'I sometimes wonder,' said Lord Dantrey, filling Diana's glass. 'You were not shocked at the scandal?'

'What scandal?' asked Diana, wide-eyed. She had only recently begun to listen to gossip, so it was possible that someone had tried to tell her the shocking on-dit about Byron and his sister during the time when she only listened to gossip about horses and dogs.

'Never mind. But to return to the question of Byron's romanticism. Now, he says he does not like women at table because he does not like to see them eat and drink for it destroys their 'etherealism' and 'romance'.

But *I* think it is because the ladies are always served first at dinner and given the wings of the chicken, of which Lord Byron is passionately fond.'

'What of Mr Brummell?'

'Alas, poor George, fled to the continent with his debtors baying at his heels. No, not romantic. Amusing, clever, sometimes cruel, but never romantic. If he had been clever enough, all the same, to keep the friendship of the Prince Regent, then I do not think his creditors would have pressed him so hard. Also, he had begun to play deep.'

'I know why the Prince Regent took him in dislike,' said Diana eagerly, 'for my sis . . . my cousin, Minerva, told me. 'Twas because he called him fat, well not direct, but to Lord Alvanley. He said, "Who's your fat friend?" '

'That happened after. He was already out of favour. The trouble, you see, was that Brummell began to believe he could say and do what he liked, eventually considering himself above Prinny. He did not realize that he was the fashion and could be terribly rude to all kinds of people simply because of Prinny's patronage. Of course, his contempt appealed to a servile streak in the top ten thousand for a certain time, but if one has no lands, no title, and very little money then one will, in the long run, need a patron, and a very powerful one at that. I was present on the evening when his downfall really started. It was at the Pavilion in Brighton. The Bishop of Winchester, a particular friend of the Regent, saw the Beau's snuff box lying on the table and helped himself to a pinch without asking Brummell's permission. Brummell turned to a servant and said in a very loud voice, "Throw that snuff into the fire or on the floor." The insult to the Regent's friend was great and the Regent was furious.'

'You must be very important to be invited to dinner by the Prince Regent.' Diana looked at him and then looked down into her wine glass. 'I have heard said, sir, that you are a rake.'

'Aha! My reputation flies before me. Perhaps I was.'

'But not now,' said Diana eagerly.

'No, not now. I am an old man, looking forward to a nursery full of squalling brats and a complacent wife on the other side of the hearth.'

'It is said you ruined some lady.'

'Young man,' said Lord Dantrey in a flat voice, 'mind your manners.'

'Oh, I am sorry, sir. There. Only see how my tongue runs away from me.' Diana looked at him, large eyes pleading for forgiveness. Those strange green and gold eyes met her own, quizzical at first and then narrowing.

'Tell me about Almack's,' said Diana breathlessly. 'I mean, *why* is it so important to go there. What *is* Almack's?'

'If you were a lady, Almack's would be important. Not to a fellow . . . unless you are seeking a rich heiress. But let me see . . . Almack's was a very clever idea from the first. A Scotsman named William McCall came to London about the middle of the last century as valet to the fifth Duke of Hamilton. He married Elizabeth Cullin, a waiting maid to the duchess. Then he was butler to Lord Bute. He then started a tavern in St James's Street, the "pickings" he had made from his previous positions providing him with the means. He prepared to call his adventure "McCall's" but was advised, owing to the unpopularity of the Scots in London just then, that this would ruin the enterprise. "Very well," said McCall, after listening to much counsel, "I will call it Almack's"—just a reversal of his name. The tavern proved a great success. He founded "Almack's Club" for gaming in Pall Mall in 1763, and a year later he built "Almack's Assembly Rooms" in King Street. It was said to be quite a sight to see McCall's Scotch face framed in a bag wig and his plump wife serving all the dukes and duchesses with tea and cakes. By clever management, he ensured that the assembly rooms should cater only to the very rich and so the rooms automatically became the home of the Exclusives. Now they have their awesome patronesses. Do you crave vouchers?'

'Not I,' said Diana, lounging back against the settle in what she hoped was a masculine manner. 'Silly little misses and their pushing mamas.'

'You are hard on the fair sex,' laughed Lord Dantrey. 'What do you wish to do now? Go to the opera?' He raised his quizzing glass and studied Diana's clothes. 'I am afraid you will need something more suitable than what you have on.'

'Could we not go somewhere a little less grand?' said Diana nervously, remembering that the Italian opera was, in its way, as exclusive as Almack's and that there was a supper and a ball after the performance.

'Very well. We shall go to the play. Finish your wine.' Lord Dantrey began to talk lightly of this and that. A shadow fell across their table as two very young men strolled past to the far end of the coffee room.

Peregrine Armitage sat down and stared at his twin, James. 'I swear upon my life that was sister Diana, dressed as a man, sitting at that table with that gentleman.'

'It *can't* be,' said James. 'The light is poor and the candle on their table was nearly burned down to the socket.' He craned his neck. 'The servant has just replaced it with a new candle. Can you see anything, Perry, without making it obvious that you're staring at them?'

'If it's her, she's got her back to me,' said Peregrine. 'I tell you what. I'll stroll over to the door and look out and then walk back.'

James waited anxiously. Peregrine slid back into his seat and ran a worried hand through his black curls. 'It's Diana all right,' he groaned. 'Putting up a good show, and she's wearing our clothes. What are we going to do? She must have gone mad.'

'Who is she with?'

'I don't know. But he's years older than her and he don't look as if he's up to any good.'

'We'd best tell father.'

'We can't tell father, you numbskull. We're supposed to be in school. If he finds out we manufactured that letter about a death in the family, he'll curse and rant and rave, fit to beat the band. Then we'll get expelled if it ever comes out.'

'Then what shall we do? It's terrible sitting here helpless while Diana behaves like Letty Lade. She must have run away from home with this man. If that's the case, he ain't respectable and he ain't got marriage in mind. Oh, what *are* we to do?'

'Tell Minerva.'

'Worse and worse. Minerva thinks we're still children. She'd march us back to school and read us a sermon at the same time. We'll write an anonymous letter to father. It is all we can do.'

'No, it's not all we can do. We will simply march up to Diana and tell her we've recognized her. She'll be in no position to report *us*.'

But when the twins went up to the table at

which Diana had been sitting, it was to find both she and her companion had left.

'Well, that's that,' said Peregrine gloomily.

'We'll send an anonymous letter to father, and then we'd best return to school as fast as we can!'

Diana found herself in the pit at Haymarket Theatre, her companion having paid the three shillings each for tickets. She shifted uneasily on her hard bench, for the fop behind her had his feet up on it. The whole theatre smelled of oranges, the old prejudice against fresh fruit being indigestible having long disappeared. Despite the fact that the oranges sold in the theatre were a ridiculous price—sixpence as opposed to the twopence halfpenny that one paid outside—everyone seemed to be buying them for the express purpose of throwing them on the stage. The play was called *The Italian Subterfuge*, but what was being said or what the whole thing was about was a mystery to Diana. The audience howled and jeered and cat-called from the rising of the curtain. Snatches of cant rose and fell about Diana as those of the audience who were not engaged in tormenting the actors gossiped loudly. 'That cover-me-decently is all very well' . . . 'pinks in Rotten Row' . . . 'the ladybirds in the saloon' . . . 'angelics of Almack's' . . . 'top of the trees' . . . 'legs and Levanters at Tattersall's' . . . 'bang-up spot of the world for fun, frolic and out-and-outing.' The top of society was referred to in various terms from roses to pink and tulips, and the lower orders as mechanical tag-rag and bobtail, vegetables, bunches of turnips, and strings of *ingyns*. Paying money conjured up many cant expressions—flash the screens, sport the rhino, show your needful, nap the rent, stump the pewter, tip the brads, and down with the dust.

Diana had several very nasty moments when they were promenading before the play started. She was accosted on all sides by prostitutes, bold and businesslike, some even presenting her with their business cards.

She decided to put her surroundings from her mind and think about Mr Jack Emberton instead. Would he call at Lady Godolphin's? Perhaps she could persuade Papa to let her return to Hopeworth for a little. This freedom, this masculine life for which she had longed, was not turning out quite the way she had expected. If only the strong,

masculine, protective figure of Jack Emberton were beside her instead of this cool and
elegant and decadent lord.

She gave a little sigh and suddenly found
her companion's eyes on her.

'Tired?'

She heard the question despite the row
going on about her, and manufactured a
yawn.

'Very,' she said. 'I am sorry to be such a
dull dog, but I confess I am weary and must
be fatiguing you with my company.'

'Not at all. Since we cannot hear what is
left of the play, I suggest we return to our
beds.'

Diana fell silent as they strolled back to
Conduit Street. Her earlier enjoyment of
Lord Dantrey's company had fled. He was
so cool and remote. She did not know what
he was thinking. She was becoming
increasingly nervous in his company. He did
not seem the type of man who would give up
his time to entertain a raw youth from a
country village. She stole a glance at him,
her eyes level with his chin. His face was
rather grim and his eyes hooded. She felt a
shiver of fear and found herself praying he
would never guess she was a girl. She toyed

with the idea of landing on Lady Godolphin's doorstep in the morning. But such a long and dreary life awaited her. There was the mysterious Jack Emberton, of course. Perhaps just one more day, thought Diana. She would escape from her overpowering companion by going out for a walk early in the morning. The streets would be quiet. No gentleman was ever seen out of doors before two.

By the time they reached the hotel, she was as tired as she had affected to be. She thanked him politely and offered to pay for her theatre ticket, an offer which he dismissed with a wave of his hand.

'We shall find something to amuse you tomorrow, Mr Armitage,' he said. 'Good night.'

Diana blushed and straightened her knees quickly, turning her curtsey into a bow.

'Good night, my lord.'

She felt his eyes on her back as she wearily mounted the dirty stairs to bed.

CHAPTER FOUR

Diana spent a restless night and awoke to the sound of the watch calling seven o'clock. The frowsty air in the room impelled her from the bed to open the window, letting in a blast of cold, sooty air.

A thin fog veiled the streets. Diana leaned her elbows on the sill. The street below was deserted. Now it would be safe to explore London, she thought. She would walk the empty streets and find that freedom for which she craved.

She made a hasty toilet and hurried down the stairs. She was hungry but meant to find breakfast at a pastry cook's when they opened.

She crossed the road from the hotel and hesitated. Which way to go?

All at once, she had a strange feeling of being watched. Diana set off at a half trot, turning right into New Bond Street, along past the shuttered shops and then right into

Oxford Street, along to High Holborn, and then towards the City where the dome of St Paul's seemed to float above the fog.

Slowly, Diana began to relax and feel more like the man she was pretending to be. A thin rain of soot was falling, making her thankful she had worn Peregrine's old blue morning coat. She tilted her hat at a rakish angle, thrust her hands in her breeches pockets and began to whistle. A cobbler was taking down the heavy wooden shutters in front of his stall. ' 'Morning, sir!' he called cheerfully, and 'Good morning!' grinned Diana, striding out in the direction of the Tower.

Sleepy servants appeared yawning on doorsteps, for they kept earlier hours in the City. Somewhere behind her came the muted clop-clop of a horse's hooves. Once or twice she turned around, but the rider was veiled in the fog.

Diana came out onto Tower Hill, near the Tower of London. She stopped short and stared with delight. Standing in front of her, on dry land, was a ship, complete with masts and rigging. As she watched, the fog thickened until it was possible to imagine the ship was riding on the sea.

She drew closer, fascinated, remembering childhood dreams of running away to sea.

'Hullo, young master.' A short, wizened little man in a travesty of a naval uniform appeared around the side of the ship. 'Would you care to come aboard and have a look around? Don't cost much.'

'How much?' asked Diana nervously. The hundred pounds which had seemed such a great sum in Hopeworth now seemed very little. Limmer's was dreadfully expensive. What on earth would she do if she were expected to gamble?

'A shilling, young master. Only a shilling. The name's Pomfret.'

'Very well, Mr Pomfret,' said Diana. 'I would very much like to see this ship of yours.'

' 'Tain't mine. Property of His Britannic Majesty's navy.'

He led the way up a gangplank. After about ten minutes' lecture, Diana came to the conclusion that Mr Pomfret must be a very lowly sort of sailor indeed, possibly confined to only one small part of the vessel, for he did not seem to know which mast was which, or even which end of the ship was the bow and which the stern.

But he told colourful tales of the time he had been taken by the pirates and Diana, who only half believed him, leaned dreamily on the rail, looking out over the billowing sea of London fog.

'Now I'll show you the men's quarters.' Mr Pomfret nipped down a companionway leading to the lower decks and Diana clattered after him, her old-fashioned square-toed boots making quite a noise on the stairs.

'First of all,' said Mr Pomfret cheerfully, 'we'll have a noggin. Here we are. My two other mates. Bosun, James Smith, and coxswain, Amos Duffy.'

The bosun and the coxswain were both squat, powerful-looking men. They were both very smelly. James Smith had one eye and Amos Duffy had one leg. Diana almost expected to find out that her guide had only one ear. She wondered wildly if the crew of this landlocked ship was made up of men with parts of their bodies missing.

All of a sudden, she wanted to leave. But Mr Pomfret had drawn up a chair for her and Amos Duffy was pouring out a glass of rum.

'Just come up from the country?' asked James Smith, clapping Diana on the back as she choked over the rum.

Diana nodded speechlessly.

'And did young master's fambly come along o' him?'

'No. I am here on my own,' said Diana.

The three men exchanged glances. 'Here, have another noggin,' cried Mr Pomfret, filling up Diana's glass again.

'I really must go,' said Diana, half rising. Amos Duffy's beefy hand pressed her back down onto her chair.

'Now then, lad. You wouldn't be offending us good gents by refusing to drink with us?'

'No, no,' bleated Diana, feeling treacherously weak and feminine. 'It's just that I . . . oh, very well. I shall drink this one glass and then I really must be on my way.'

The rum burned its way down to her empty stomach and the fumes rose to her brain, dulling some of her inexplicable fear. For what on earth could happen to her on Tower Hill in the very heart of London?

Mr Pomfret hitched his chair closer to Diana's. 'I'll tell you something, young master,' he leered. 'Blessed if I can remember when I took such a fancy to a young man. So here's what I'm going to do.' He fumbled in his greasy waistcoat, extracted a shilling and held it up. 'This here shilling wot you gave me, I'm giving it back. Here, take it.'

'No, please keep it, Mr Pomfret,' said Diana.

'Take it or we'll be mortal offended,' growled Amos Duffy.

Diana looked helplessly from one to the other and then took the shilling. 'Now, if you will excuse me . . .' she rose determinedly to her feet.

'Sit down!' barked Mr Pomfret. 'Welcome to the King's navy, lad.'

'I d-don't understand,' said Diana.

'That waur the King's shilling you took. So you're in the navy now, lad!'

Diana sank down in her chair and blinked back the rush of tears to her eyes. She was a flat, a gull, a country turnip.

She, Diana Armitage, had been press-ganged!

Fear cancelled out the effects of the rum. Her large eyes looked to left and right, calculating her chances of escape. Amos Duffy had risen and was standing between her and the door. James Smith had a large horse pistol sticking up conspicuously out of the top of one sea boot.

What if she should reveal the fact that she was a woman? But Diana dismissed that thought almost as soon as it was formed. She was sure the three men would be delighted to play another sort of game with her.

And then a light step sounded on the deck above.

'Help!' screamed Diana. 'Help me!'

'Stow your racket.' The pistol was pressed to her ear. 'Tie him up and put a gag in his mouth,' growled Amos. 'You gets above, Pomfret, and see who's about.'

Diana was gagged and bound and dragged over to a corner, tossed in it face down, and covered with a blanket.

She lay shaking with fear. Prayers tumbled out against the gag. God was punishing her for betraying her sex. For the first time, Diana realized the full enormity of what she had done. She had fled her respectable home to consort with a famous rake. She had brought ruin on the Armitage family. All she could pray was that these ruffians would not guess she was a lady until she could manage to get the ear of some officer. For if they discovered her sex, Diana was convinced they would rape her first and kill her afterwards.

Her muffled prayers, she was sure, were rising up above the masts of the ship, above the London fog to the ears of a harsh God who would probably not lift a finger to save her since everyone knew you had to be punished for your sins.

And then she heard a familiar voice. Light, cool and drawling, Lord Dantrey was audible outside the room, saying, 'It is no use cringing and leering at me, Mr Pomfret—if that is your name. I am no country lad to be pressganged by such as you. I am convinced you have my ward here. And if you have, I shall see to it that you are put in the pillory at Charing Cross along with whoever is in this business with you.

'Or, if I can put it in a more delicate manner, produce my ward, Mr Armitage, this instant or I will blow your evil brains out.'

Diana heard the hammer of a pistol cock. She tried to cry out against the tightness of the gag.

She wrenched herself over on her side, dislodging the blanket from her face so that she could see what was going on in the room. Amos was standing behind the door with a stout stick raised in both hands. His intention was obviously to club down Lord Dantrey as soon as he appeared through the door. Her eyes enormous in her white face, Diana kicked blindly with her bound legs, trying to do something to take Amos' attention away from the door.

The door swung open. Lord Dantrey swung about and seized Mr Pomfret by the collar of his pea jacket and thrust him forwards into the room, and Amos brought the club fairly and squarely down on the unlucky Mr Pomfret's head. Mr Smith rushed forward but halted at the sight of the pistol in Lord Dantrey's hand.

Lord Dantrey's eyes fell on the four glasses on the table and then roamed over the room, finally noticing the wriggling figure in the dark corner.

'Go and untie him.' Lord Dantrey waved the pistol at Amos. Grumbling about only doing the King's duty, Amos set about freeing Diana. 'Come here and stand behind me, Mr Armitage,' ordered Lord Dantrey. Diana stumbled to her feet, clutching hold of the table to get her balance.

'Now, gentlemen,' said Lord Dantrey, 'sit

down at that table and do not dare move an inch. I shall lock you in as a precaution. Mr Armitage, pray relieve Mr Whateverhisnameis of that nasty looking pistol. You will find it in his boot. You should have fired at me as I came through the door, not tried to club me. Thank you, Mr Armitage. Let us go.' Drawing Diana with him, Lord Dantrey retreated into the corridor and locked the door behind him.

'Not a word, Mr Armitage,' he said coldly. 'You may explain yourself when we return to Limmer's.'

Still, Diana tried to babble her thanks, but he would not listen. He mounted his horse and pulled her up behind him. 'It was you who was following me,' said Diana to his well-tailored back, but he did not reply, setting a steady pace out of the City towards the West End.

Diana was not very afraid of Lord Dantrey's temper. She had been tricked like any greenhorn, but she had told Lord Dantrey that she, David Armitage, lacked town bronze. Also, he was not her father and so he could not strike her or beat her in any way.

When they had dismounted and the ostler

had taken Lord Dantrey's horse round to the mews, Lord Dantrey looked down at Diana and said quietly, 'Let us go to your room.'

Lord Dantrey's face was white against the fog and his eyes were like chips of emerald set in gold.

Diana folded her lips in a mutinous line. It had been clever of him to claim her as his ward. But he had no authority over her. She was her own mistress—master. She would *not* be bullied. Surely, anyone who had survived the lash of the vicar's tongue on the hunting field could cope with anyone else's sermonizing.

But her knees trembled when they were finally upstairs in her room. For the first time in her young life, Diana began to think that the lot of a female was not *quite* so unhappy. Women were not pressganged. They were not expected to gamble for vast sums of money, or drink heavily, or fight for their lives.

Lord Dantrey drew off his York tan gloves and placed his hat and cane on the table beside the bed. Despite the cold of the morning he, like Diana, had not put on a top coat. Even the normally democratic London soot had left his cravat shining white. Diana had seen fair-haired people whose locks glinted with silver, but his almost white hair glinted with threads of gold which was . . .

'Well, Mr Armitage?'

'It was very kind of you to rescue me,' said Diana, her voice made gruff with embarrassment. 'I was caught like the veriest flat. But how was I to know that such practises would be condoned in full daylight on a ship that appears to have been built for no other purpose than pressganging.'

'They do not often run up against trouble,' said Lord Dantrey. 'They make very sure of their target. The shabbiness of that disgusting coat added to the fact that you no doubt told them you had come up from the country made them feel you were an easy mark. It was as well I followed you. I shall put a token protest to the authorities, but I doubt if they will give it much heed.'

'It's disgraceful,' said Diana. 'But why did you follow me, my lord?'

'Because I was already regretting having invited you to London. Also, it is a long time since I have held a woman in my arms and I am not one to scorn such easy pickings . . . *Miss Armitage.*'

'You *know?*'

'From almost the first. You must be Diana.'

Diana miserably hung her head.

'I thought so. You are too old to be Frederica and the four married ones are famous for their beauty' . . . Diana winced . . . 'and for the great love they have for their respective husbands. Why do you masquerade as a man?'

'Because I have a great love of the chase,' said Diana, sitting down in a chair beside the bedroom fire. 'Papa said I might hunt provided I disguised myself.'

'Shocking, but understandable,' he said, coming to stand over her. 'But what of the rest? Where does your father believe you to be?'

'With Lady Godolphin in Hanover Square. You see, I arrived there and pretended to be my own servant. Although I was supposed to arrive last Wednesday, I altered Papa's letter so she does not expect me until *next* Wednesday. I am . . . you see, it is all very hard to explain. I am to make my come-out next Season and Lady Godolphin is to teach me how to go on. I dread the thought of wearing silly gowns and simpering and flirting and not ever again being able to hunt. No one knew I had been at your home. There was no scandal. I only wanted one week of freedom.'

'And what is wrong with finding a husband and bearing his children? Women are fit for naught else.'

'They *must* be. There must be more to life for a woman than a life given over to triviality.'

'Most of the gentlemen at this hotel,' he said drily, 'live lives completely given up to pleasure. Had you, Miss Diana, been born into a lower order of society, then you would have had to work from sun-up to sundown. The fact that the good Lord has seen fit to put you in a higher station should be enough for you. Think you not that the scullery maid does not envy the ladies who go to balls and routs dressed in their finest?'

'I can ride better than most men,' said Diana. 'And my father taught me to fish and shoot.'

'Then, what would you? Do you wish to become one of the half creatures, neither fish nor fowl? Shame on you, Miss Diana. Stand up!'

Diana miserably rose to her feet and he seized her by the shoulders and twisted her about so that she was facing the mirror above the mantle.

'Look!' he said. 'Neither handsome man nor pretty woman. Look, Miss Diana Armitage.'

Diana looked. Her rough-cut hair was standing out around her face in spiky curls. Soot had blackened her nose at either side of her nostrils and her cravat was a limp, soot-spotted rag. There was a smut of soot on her forehead. She wrenched herself out of his grasp and went and washed her face at the toilet table, noticing, despite her humiliation and misery, that flecks of soot were floating in the washing water.

She scrubbed her face dry with a towel and then turned to face him, some of her courage returning. 'If,' she said coldly, 'you knew me to be a woman, then why did you keep up the pretence? Why do you think I sought your company?'

He smiled, a wicked glint in his eyes.

'I thought the reasons obvious, Miss Armitage. I have possessed a considerable fortune for some time. I am used to all the subterfuges to trap me into marriage. I merely thought this one was more original than the others.'

'You conceited coxcomb,' said Diana, outraged. 'You thought that *I* had a *tendre* for *you.*'

'It has been known.'

'Insufferable!' Beside herself with rage, Diana crossed the room and slapped him full in the face.

He clipped her arms behind her back and held her against him so tightly she could feel the beating of his heart.

He moved his face down towards her own.

'No!' said Diana, twisting this way and that. She was a powerful girl and it was terrifying to find herself so helpless, to find how easily he could pin her against him with one hand. His mouth came down on hers. Her whole body shook and trembled with outrage. Then she decided the best thing to do was to stay still. But her trembling increased and he raised his mouth and looked down at her with a teasing smile. 'Oh, Diana,' he said huskily, and bent his head to hers again.

Diana marshalled all her strength and brought one foot shod in a clumsy, heavy boot with full force down on his toes. He released her with a yelp of agony.

'Go, sir!' said Diana, white with rage.

'Don't ever look at me or speak to me again.'

He took a step towards her and she grabbed the remains of the washing water and threw the contents full in his face. Then she nipped past him and hurtled down the stairs, careering off the bannister in her headlong flight. The clerk stared amazed as she shot past him and out into the street. She ran blindly, desperately, until she was sure he was not in pursuit. It was then that she found herself in Hanover Square. She looked down at her masculine clothes and shuddered. Never again would she wear them.

She must throw herself on Lady Godolphin's mercy.

Diana marched up to the door of Lady Godolphin's imposing mansion and rang the bell. She announced herself, hopefully for the very last time, as David Armitage. Mice, the butler, cast a cold eye over her soiled and rumpled clothes, but said he would see if my lady was awake.

Heart beating hard, Diana sat in a hard chair in the hall. Over and over again she rehearsed her speech, and her lips were moving soundlessly when Mice at last returned to lead her upstairs to my lady's bedchamber.

'Who are you?' demanded Lady Godolphin crossly, struggling up against the pillows. 'Don't know any David Armitage.'

Diana did not reply. She turned and looked at Mice, patently waiting for the butler to leave.

'Oh, go on,' said Lady Godolphin to her butler. 'He obviously ain't going to state his business with you in the room.' Mice cast one suspicious look at Diana and went out and closed the door.

'Now, young man,' said Lady Godolphin.

Diana began to cry. Great tears rolled down her cheeks. 'I'm Diana Armitage,' she wailed. 'Oh, Lady Godolphin, what am I to *do?*'

'Gad's Hounds!' said Lady Godolphin, getting out of bed. 'Sit down and calm yourself. What a way for a miss to go on.'

Diana gulped and sobbed but managed to choke out the whole story. Lady Godolphin sat down by the fire and rested her heavy chin in her hand. She had not removed her paint the night before and her bulldog face peered out from under a thick thatch of a red wig. Pulling on what she described as a peeingnoir, Lady Godolphin rang for her maid.

'I will read you a sermon later, Diana,' she said. 'At this moment, the best thing I can do is to try and salvage your reputation. I shall call on this Dantrey at Limmer's and make sure he's going to keep his mouth closed. How on earth your father did not guess what you were about is beyond me. You will go to bed and sleep and we shall decide what's to be done after that. I have a new maid, good at her job, but stupid. Nothing ever seems to surprise her. She won't make comment.'

The maid, Sally, was a thin, wiry, middle-aged woman whose nut-cracker face was screwed up into permanent lines of simpering gentility. She was told to put Miss Diana to bed and to return to prepare her mistress for the street.

All this the maid did with many arch winks and grimaces. Diana, despite her misery, wondered if Sally were quite sane. But it was wonderful to sink into a soft feather bed, the scallop-shaped bed which had so shocked Minerva on her first visit to London, and snuggle down into sheets heated by the warming pan. Diana's last thought before she fell asleep was one of gratitude that she had such an unconventional chaperone.

'Lady to see you, my lord,' said the hotel servant with a cheeky grin which quickly faded before the icy look in Lord Dantrey's eyes.

'Show her up,' said Lord Dantrey. So she had come back. He might have known. Any girl who dressed as a man and flouted the conventions so blatantly must have the morals of a tom cat.

He walked to the door and looked along the corridor. Two large zebra striped feathers followed by a hideous scarlet turban followed by Lady Godolphin's pugnacious face rose jerkily into view.

Lord Dantrey swore under his breath. So Diana was not so green. He was about to be blackmailed into marriage.

'Well, don't just stand there,' snapped Lady Godolphin as soon as she saw him. 'You're Dantrey by the looks of you. What I've got to say is personal.'

'I have no doubt,' said Lord Dantrey grimly, standing aside to let her pass.

Lady Godolphin's faded blue eyes raked up and down the length of Lord Dantrey's elegant figure. Then she plumped herself down in an armchair.

'Sit down,' she said, 'and don't loom over me. Diana's with me and crying her eyes out. Why were you party to the silly girl's deceit? There's plenty of lightskirts in London. What made ye think a vicar's daughter was for sport?'

Lord Dantrey sat down opposite her and stretched out his long legs. 'When a girl behaves as boldly as Diana Armitage, I assume she knows what she is about. She cannot possibly have expected me to believe her a man.'

'She seems to have gulled most,' said Lady Godolphin. 'You've got a bad reputation, Dantrey, but I thought that was only the mud of some youthful folly still sticking to you. You're old enough to know better.'

'It is no use forcing me into marriage . . .'

'No one wants you to marry the girl. Far from it. Unless you've taken her vaginal.'

'Lady Godolphin!'

'Aye, well, she said you hadn't. Only kissed her. Why I am here is to see the matter goes no further. You keep quiet, Diana keeps quiet, and no more will be said.'

'I confess I am relieved,' said Lord Dantrey, looking curiously at Lady Godolphin. 'You may think my behaviour odd, but then I have heard some very warm tales of the Armitage girls on my travels. There was a certain Mr Hugh Fresne who implied they were all lightskirts . . .'

'Ah, that coxcomb. Minerva made a fool of him.'

'And then when I was in Virginia, Mr Guy Wentwater said the sisters were better hunters than the father when it came to catching a rich husband. He said certain things . . .'

'You keep low company,' snapped Lady Godolphin. 'All these gels are as pure as the driven lambs. Wentwater has a black past. Neither of those charlatans would dare say such things in England. You have not answered me direct. Will you keep quiet about Diana's masquerade and will you keep away from her?'

'You may have my oath on that,' he said. 'What a termagant!'

'She is a shocked and frightened little girl.'

'She is a giantess who not only stamped on my feet but threw water in my face.'

'Bags of spirit,' grinned Lady Godolphin, getting to her feet. She looked up at him curiously. 'You recognized me immediately. Did we ever meet?'

Lord Dantrey's lips twitched. He had never actually been introduced to Lady Godolphin—but what member of the top ten thousand did not know that outlandish-looking lady by sight? 'I have long admired you from afar,' he said, bowing from the waist.

Lady Godolphin gave her largest crocodile-like smile. Lord Dantrey wondered if her lip rouge ever stained her ear lobes.

'You don't have the manner of a rake,' said Lady Godolphin. 'Ain't heard of you playing the fool or going on debauched sprees. I 'member now. It was a certain Miss Blessington you wouldn't marry when folks said you ought.'

'I should really send you packing and tell you to mind your own business,' said Lord Dantrey. 'Miss Blessington, as you may know, is now happily married with a nursery full of children. The fact is, she set a trap for me and I was young and gullible. I knew, too late, her family had aided and abetted her with an eye to my fortune and a desire to add my name to that of their own undistin-guished tree. So I refused to marry her. I preferred to take the blame. One mistake,' he said bitterly, 'and it seems destined to damn my reputation for life.'

'But did you not think you might find yourself in the same position with Diana? Why on earth did you encourage the girl in such folly?'

Lord Dantrey looked into the glowing embers of the fire. Why had he done such a thing? Because he had been bored and she had come out of the storm, fresh and wild. Because she did not seem to be governed by any conventional laws. Because what he had heard of the Armitages led him to believe them unconventional, to say the least. And because he had been so sure she would have covered her tracks and he had longed for the week's escapade as much as she had done. Aloud he said, 'Folly. Mere folly. Let us be thankful that that is the end of it and no harm done.'

'It's a pity,' leered Lady Godolphin, 'for you've a good leg on you.' Lord Dantrey blinked. 'Just like my Arthur, although he's thinner in the calf.'

'Your husband?'

'No. My sissybeau.'

'Cicisbeo?'

'Him. He was. Now he ain't and more's the pity.'

Lord Dantrey shook his head as if to clear it. 'Pray forgive me for not offering you any refreshment, Lady Godolphin. Would you like some tea?'

'Not here,' said Lady Godolphin with a shudder. 'Pooh, 'tis filthy. Good day to you, my lord. I'll have Miss Diana married before the Season begins. Look how well I did for the other girls!'

Lord Dantrey watched her until the feathers and then the turban disappeared down the stairs. He was well rid of Miss Diana Armitage. He shrugged and confessed to himself he had got off lightly. He turned and walked to the window and stared out into the thick fog, seeing only his own reflection in the dirty glass. All at once it seemed a very good idea to go to his club and get thoroughly drunk.

A week had passed since Diana's adventure. Neither she nor Lady Godolphin went out much since the town was thin of company. Diana found herself enjoying the staid uneventfulness of it all. By an effort of will she had pushed all thoughts of the horrible Lord Dantrey from her mind. Minerva confided to Lady Godolphin that she was delighted with the change in her hoydenish younger sister.

And then, just as Diana was preparing to go driving with Lady Godolphin, Sally scratched at the door and called out that there was a gentleman waiting belowstairs to see Miss Diana. Diana's heart began to hammer against her ribs. Dantrey! It could not be anyone else. She had not met any gentlemen, since her outings had been confined to visits to Minerva and to Lady Godolphin's circle of elderly friends.

She searched her face in the glass to make sure there were no traces of David Armitage. She must look every inch a lady in order to keep Lord Dantrey at a distance. Her hair grew quickly and Sally's clever fingers had done wonders with it. Diana was wearing a carriage dress consisting of a Russian mantle of pomona sarsnet trimmed with rich frog fringe. A bonnet with a tall crown framed her face and she wore slippers of green kid on her feet.

Confident that she looked every inch a gentlewoman, Diana went downstairs with her head held high. What on earth had possessed Lady Godolphin to grant Lord Dantrey an audience?

But it was not Lord Dantrey who was waiting for her in the Green Saloon, but Mr Jack Emberton, resplendent in elegant morning dress, his boots polished to a mirror shine and his black curls cut à la Brutus.

Diana blushed and sank into a curtsey. 'Mr Emberton says he has met you before,' said Lady Godolphin. 'He has taken the Wentwater place.'

'I know,' smiled Diana. 'What brings you to London, Mr Emberton?'

'Because a certain attraction I hoped to find in Hopeworth was no longer there,' said Mr Emberton, his blue eyes twinkling. 'I found out that much when I was hunting with your father.'

'Oh!' Diana clasped her hands. 'How did the hunt go? Did Papa catch that old fox that has been plaguing him so?'

'I am afraid not, Miss Diana, but we had some famous sport, nonetheless. Do you drive with me? I shall tell you all about it. Lady Godolphin has given her permission.'

'I would be honoured, sir,' said Diana with a demure curtsey while Lady Godolphin beamed her approval. Diana appeared to be turning out the easiest mannered of all the sisters.

As Mr Emberton helped Diana up into his phaeton, she could not help noticing that his horses were poor showy things, and charitably assumed he had rented them. His driving proved to be equally showy, but he had such merry eyes and such a deep, rumbling infectious laugh that Diana found herself enjoying the outing as she had never enjoyed any outing before. She could not help noticing the admiring glances thrown at him by the other ladies in the Park. He was so very large and broad-shouldered that he made her feel deliciously small and feminine. Now, Lord Dantrey was tall and broad-shouldered but his bearing was cool and sophisticated whereas Mr Emberton had such free and easy manners. He treated her as a lady and yet he treated her as an equal. And he talked hunting. He talked with such fluency and descriptive detail that Diana's heart warmed to him. Here was a man who would be a *companion*. Here was the masculine friendship for which she had craved. She had been a silly goose to think she had to behave like a man to have the friendship of a man. The glow of admiration in Mr Emberton's eyes warmed away the humiliation inflicted on her by Lord Dantrey.

For his part, Mr Emberton found himself enjoying Diana's company. He decided his best plan of campaign was an old and tried one which had succeeded before. He would get Diana to fall in love with him. He would propose marriage, and then he would tell that worldly and ambitious vicar that he, Jack Emberton, had neither money nor prospects. The vicar would then surely raise enough money from his in-laws to pay the dangerous Mr Emberton to go away. That way he would have the money without any loss of reputation. He would be regarded as the injured party and he meant to play his part of being in love with Diana to the hilt. Mr Emberton had never been in love—he loved himself too much to waste that tender emotion on anyone else. But he had to admit, as he looked at Diana's glowing face, that she affected his senses as no woman had done before.

A vision of the gypsy woman's face arose before Diana's eyes. She was not yet in love with Mr Emberton but she knew it was only a matter of time. She thanked God for her deliverance from the rakish Lord Dantrey and for having been forgiven her sins in such a pleasant way.

'It's been said you hunt with your father,' said Mr Emberton.

'Indeed?' said Diana. 'Only look how cold and bare the trees seem. On a day like this one would think summer would never, ever return.' Diana was not about to tell Mr Emberton of her masquerade. He might prove shocked, and he might form such a low opinion of her morals that he would go away and she would never see him again.

'Very cold,' he agreed. So she did not want to reply to his question. That meant she *did* hunt with her father. 'That Wentwater place is as cold as charity as well,' he went on easily. 'I don't think the building's been properly fired this age.'

'Lady Wentwater disappeared some time ago,' said Diana, frowning as she remembered snatches of whispered conversation which had indicated that Lady Wentwater was not a lady, with or without a capital L. 'Did you see her when you arranged the rental of the house?'

'No, it was done through an agent in Hopeminster who was doing it for an agent in Bristol. Mortal cheap it was. I got a bargain,' said Mr Emberton with unconscious vulgarity.

'Do you return to Hopeworth soon?' asked Diana.

He looked at her out of the corner of his eyes in a calculating way. It would be better if he could lure Miss Armitage back to the country. It was silly to pay rent for a house in the country and rent for lodgings in town as well. He meant to make as much profit out of this game as possible.

Just then a black cat ran across in front of the carriage. Diana let out a cry of alarm.

'I wasn't within an ace of touching the thing,' said Mr Emberton.

'It was not that. It's very unlucky, you see,' said Diana earnestly. 'Some people think it lucky when a black cat crosses their path but I hold the other view.'

'That's only superstition,' laughed Mr Emberton.

'I think a great number of these old superstitions are very wise,' said Diana, becomingly increasingly upset. 'Oh, I do wish that cat had not appeared!'

'I'm a very lucky person,' said Mr Emberton. 'Pooh to all black cats. I shall guard you from all supernatural curses, including the evil eye.'

'You are mocking me.'

'Not I. I think that cat was a sign you should return to Hopeworth. We could ride together.'

Diana closed her eyes for a moment as she had a blissful vision of riding before the wind, shoulder to shoulder with this handsome man.

She opened them again and let out a little squeak of alarm. Approaching them, in a smart turnout, came Lord Dantrey and a male friend.

'Now what?' demanded her companion, amused. 'I know. You've seen the Witch of Endor.'

'Not that,' said Diana in a small voice. 'I think I should like to return home.'

'Very well,' he said, 'but on one condition. You must tell me when I may enjoy the pleasure of your company again or I shall bring all sorts of curses down upon your beautiful head.'

Diana laughed, suddenly carefree, as the carriage turned about and headed through the Park in the direction of the north gate.

Lord Dantrey watched them go. So Miss

Diana had found herself a beau, and very quickly too.

'Who was the beauty?' demanded his friend, Mr Tony Fane. 'I see you were much struck by her as well.'

'Beauty?' said Lord Dantrey, not wanting to admit to himself that he had been startled by Diana's appearance. 'A trifle too bold and gypsyish for my taste. I believe her to be one of the Armitage girls.'

'Ah, the famous Armitage girls. That explains it. Did you ever see such a stable of beauties? And all different. I might try my luck in that direction.'

Lord Dantrey was normally very fond of the easy-going Mr Fane but he found himself suddenly out of charity with him. 'If you are going to chase after every petticoat in London,' he said acidly, 'then I fear I must do without the pleasure of your company.'

'Faith! Your spleen must be disordered. I did not say *every* petticoat in London, merely one very respectable and beautiful petticoat. What could be more *convenable* than a vicar's daughter?'

'From what I have heard of the good vicar, he is anything but religious. Ambition and money are his gods. Who was that fellow with Miss Armitage?'

'Ah, I was coming to that. Jack Emberton is his name and he makes a living at the card tables. He always gets some well-connected weakling to introduce him to other well-connected weaklings and then fleeces 'em at the tables.'

'Then what is his interest in Miss Armitage? I do not believe the family to be very rich although I suppose they are well-connected by marriage.'

'You have been away in foreign parts too long. You have forgot the charm of a genuine English beauty. Don't need to be interested in money to be interested in Miss Armitage.'

Lord Dantrey found himself prey to an impulse to ride to Hanover Square and warn Lady Godolphin of the unsavoury company her charge was keeping. Then he shrugged. A girl who would dress as a man, stamp rudely on his feet, and throw water in his face was no doubt a match for Jack Emberton.

He decided to return to his solitude in the country soon. London was so full of upsetting people!

And she *had* noticed him. But all she had

done was to close her eyes as if she had seen some horror.

The Reverend Charles Armitage was dancing up and down on the doorstep when Squire Jimmy Radford opened the door.

'Charles!' exclaimed the squire. 'Come in. Come in. Ram is about somewhere and will fetch us some wine. I have a very good . . .'

'I'll never touch wine again,' howled the vicar.

'Oh, dear,' said the squire. 'It must be serious.' He led the way into the library. Ram, his Indian servant, came in, and the squire ordered tea.

The vicar sank into a chair beside the fire and buried his head in his hands. 'God is punishing me,' he mumbled.

The little squire, who thought that Charles Armitage often did a very good job of setting up situations to punish himself without any help from his Maker, forbore from saying so.

The squire judged that one of the vicar's daughters was in trouble and that the vicar blamed himself for that trouble. Charles Armitage, faced with any nasty consequences brought about by parental neglect, always started by swearing to give up something

119

—his hunt, his religion, his wine or his food.

The vicar tugged a grimy letter out of his capacious pocket and handed it to the squire.

The squire took it and looked at it with distaste. It was made up of letters cut from the newspapers. It read, 'Yr daughter, Diana, has been seen dressed as a man being entertained by an evil-looking rake in Hubbold's coffee house. A friend.'

'But this cannot be true,' said the squire. 'A nasty anonymous letter! Diana is with Lady Godolphin. Did you not question your servants?'

The vicar nodded. 'John Summer said he delivered her right to the door. Sarah saw her in as well, but Sarah was sulky because Diana sent her straight back and would not even allow the girl an hour in London to see the shops.'

'Then what ails you? It is upsetting in a way to think that someone might know that Diana Armitage, has been in the habit of masquerading as a man. The rest is lies.'

'I know it's not,' said the vicar, striking his waistcoat. 'I feel it here.' He looked pleadingly at the squire. 'I can't sit waiting for a reply to any letter I send to Lady Godolphin. I mean to leave today and travel to London . . .'

'And you want me to go with you,' said the squire gently.

'Would you, Jimmy? It would be like old times, setting things to rights together.'

'Of course I will go with you.' The squire sighed a little and looked out at the steel grey coldness of the day and wished he did not have to leave his comfortable fireside.

'Hey, I feel better already,' grinned the vicar. 'You're a tonic, Jimmy.'

Ram came in and started to lift cannisters of tea out of the teapoy. The vicar watched in amazement.

'What's he doing?'

'Ram? He is merely making tea for us, Charles.'

'Tea! Pah! When did I ever want tea?'

'My dear Charles, you did say you would never touch wine again.'

'Oh, ah.' The vicar gave an uneasy, baffled look in the direction of the teapoy. Then his face cleared. 'I didn't say nothing about *brandy*,' he said triumphantly.

'Brandy, please, Ram,' said the squire. 'Perhaps you would like to make a call with me, Charles. I feel we should pay a visit to Lord Dantrey. He does not go out much and he is reported to have been ill. He had a somewhat unsavoury reputation as a rake, but that was when he was a very young man. Diana is in London and Frederica safely in the seminary, so you have no chicks to protect friom this wicked lord. I think if we left in the morning for London it would be time enough.'

Ram poured a large glass of brandy and set it on a little table beside the vicar. The wind howled in the chimney and rattled the bare branches of the trees outside.

'Very well,' said the vicar, beginning to feel all his worries about Diana had been groundless. 'You know, it's a pity in a way that I bundled Diana off to London. That Jack Emberton what's taken Lady Went-water's place seems a regular out-and-outer. Seemed much taken with Diana. Said he met her just as she was setting out for London.'

'Nothing is known of Mr Emberton,' said the squire cautiously, 'although I admit he seems a very straightforward sort of young man.'

The two friends set out on horseback an hour later, riding across the fields in the direction of the old Osbadiston house.

They were received by the butler, Chalmers, who informed them that his lordship had left for London. He offered them refreshment, which the two refused, being now anxious to return and begin their preparations for the journey to London.

They were just turning to leave when Chalmers said, 'I believe his lordship went to join your relative, Mr Armitage.'

The vicar stood as if turned to stone.

'What relative?' asked the squire.

'Why, Mr David Armitage, sir. He arrived here on the night of the storm, having lost his way.'

The vicar pulled himself together with a visible effort. 'This David Armitage,' he said. 'I can't call him to mind . . .'

'Oh, sir, I overheard the young gentleman say he was visiting you at the vicarage.'

'Tall fellow, was he?' demanded the vicar breathlessly. 'Tall with black hair and a sort of girlish look about him—wearing a scarlet hunting coat?'

'The very same, sir.'

'Let us go, Charles,' said the squire quickly, seeing the vicar looking ready to explode.

They rode silently away until they were

clear of the house.

'I'll kill her,' growled the vicar.

'It may not be as bad as it seems, Charles,' said the squire, although he looked as if he were trying to reassure himself. 'It was a terrible storm, and you were so very angry. It would be only natural for Diana to lose her way and to seek shelter at the nearest house. It seems this Lord Dantrey did not know Diana was a woman. We shall not worry until we see Lady Godolphin.

'I am persuaded we shall find Diana surrounded by a court of young men. She will already have forgotten her hunting days.

'There is nothing to worry about. Of that I am sure. Nothing to worry about at all.'

CHAPTER FIVE

Lady Godolphin was well content. Charles Armitage had paid up handsomely on the previous occasions when she had been successful in arranging marriages for his daughters and she had every expectation that he would prove equally generous after Mr Jack Emberton asked for Diana's hand in marriage. Lady Godolphin quite forgot that the Armitage sisters had managed to ensnare husbands largely without her help and that she had not really been instrumental in bringing Mr Emberton and Diana together.

Mr Emberton was a fine specimen of manhood, thought Lady Godolphin, looking fondly at that young man over the dinner table. Mr Emberton was intent on demolishing a hedgehog, that popular dessert made from six eggs, a quart of almonds and a pint of cream. He finished every last morsel, licked the spoon, and leaned back in his chair giving a hearty belch. Lady

Godolphin smiled her approval at the compliment to her table, but Diana flinched. She could never quite get used to gentlemen giving a hearty belch as a mark of approval. Lord Dantrey did not belch. Lord Dantrey was made of ice. 'Fire and ice,' said a treacherous little voice in her head. His lips had burned. She shook her head impatiently and her long pearl earrings, a present from Annabelle, swayed against her cheek.

Despite her happiness in Mr Emberton's company, despite that warm feeling of standing on the threshold of love, Diana was prey to a twinge of unease, almost a feeling of discontent. She remembered being happy as a child, a different sort of happiness, not this confused mixture of elation and alarm. How long and sunny and simple the days of youth seemed, thought Diana, feeling ninety. Perhaps growing up meant one could never again be happy in an uncomplicated way. There was no way back down the long road to childhood where summers were always golden and sunny, and the winters snowy and shining white.

Then, as one grew in size, adults no longer seemed like confident giants to be trusted and obeyed. Diana had never believed that one lived happily ever after once one was married. Annabelle had thrown a vase at her husband's head one day and had shouted terrible things at him. Admittedly, the next day she had been laughing and affectionate, but Diana had felt Annabelle should not have quarrelled with her husband at all. Minerva was happy. But Minerva had always been happy, thought Diana naively, and she had always played 'mother' to the rest of them, so it followed that marriage should simply be an extension of her vicarage life.

She did not see much of Deirdre and Daphne, but the last time she had seen Daphne that beautiful matron had had a severe toothache, and the last time she had seen Deirdre, that normally sparkling and vital creature had cried all day over the death of one of her kitchen maids. It was not that one should not cry, but novels always seemed to stop at the wedding. Perhaps it was because no one wanted to know what went on after the wedding, or perhaps everyone *did* know that the first blissful rapture faded into tolerance, punctuated with babies.

'Diana!' Lady Godolphin's voice penetrated her muddled thoughts. 'Colonel Brian is speaking to you.'

'I was merely asking whether Miss Diana was looking forward to her first Season,' said the colonel.

'Yes,' said Diana politely. 'There will be many balls and parties.'

Colonel Brian was even greyer than when Diana had last seen him, which was in the heydey of the colonel's affair with Lady Godolphin. Diana was not shocked at the thought of two such elderly people having an affair. Once over forty, an affair was surely a tonnish name for companionship.

'Miss Diana is not looking forward to the Season at all,' laughed Jack Emberton. 'Miss Diana would rather be on horseback riding across the moors above Hopeworth.'

Diana gave him a quick smile. 'I must put away those days, Mr Emberton,' she said. 'It would be arrogance to think myself beyond coping with the rigours of the Season when every gently-bred lady has to do the same thing.'

'Ah, but the ladies "do" the Season to find a husband, Miss Diana. What if you were to find a husband *before* the Season, some man who would let you ride free to your heart's content?'

Diana coloured faintly and studied her plate.

'That was a bit warm,' whispered Colonel Brian in Lady Godolphin's ear. 'Have you checked out this man's background?'

'Yes,' lied Lady Godolphin impatiently. Like most people who pride themselves on being good judges of character, Lady Godolphin remembered only the few times she had been right about someone and forgot all the times she had been wrong.

Mr Emberton was so *solid*, so well-dressed, so comfortable a man to have at the dinner table, it stood to reason he must have an impeccable background. In truth, Lady Godolphin found the Armitage sons-in-law a trifle overwhelming. She liked her men to be a little more earthy, and she flushed with pleasure as Colonel Brian pressed her hand under the table. She had often tried to reanimate their early affair, but when she wanted it back, the colonel seemed to have grown cold, and when *he* wanted to do something about it, Lady Godolphin somehow treated him coldly, feeling obliged to pay him off for past rejections.

The rest of the evening proceeded

amicably. Since there were only the four of them, the gentlemen did not wish to be left with their wine but begged the ladies to stay at table and continue talking. The candles burned low in their sockets. Diana listened to Mr Emberton's easy voice, talking of this and that, and dreamed of being on a more intimate footing with him so that she could learn more of his adventurous life. He did not actually *say* much, seeming happy to describe other people's adventures and stories. He appeared to know all the rich and famous people in London with the exception of Diana's brothers-in-law. Then, just as Lady Godolphin was about to bring the evening to an end, Mr Emberton said, 'I hear Dantrey has come back to this country.'

Diana's face became set. Lady Godolphin said hurriedly, 'I must tell the servants to buy the milk from the cows in Green Park and not from those wretched Welsh milk-maids who come to the doorstep. I don't know what that blueish fluid is supposed to be, but it's certainly not milk.'

Diana began to talk quickly of various interesting and amusing hawkers, her voice breathless and rapid.

'Oho!' thought Mr Emberton. 'A mystery

here.' But he did not mention Lord Dantrey again that evening.

As he was waiting for Colonel Brian to be helped into his greatcoat, Mr Emberton murmured to Diana, 'I fear you do not like London. Would you like me to try to persuade your father to let you return to Hopeworth?'

Diana clasped her hands and looked at him with wide beseeching eyes. 'I should like that of all things,' she said.

He raised her hand to his lips and looked into her wide dark eyes. Diana quickly withdrew her hand and buried it in the folds of her dress. She smiled at him to cover her rudeness. But there had been something almost predatory in his eyes, in his bearing, that had made her instinctively shrink from him. She put it down quickly to a normal female nervousness in the face of the attentions of such a masculine man.

When she was being undressed for bed by Sally, Lady Godolphin's maid, Diana pondered over the strangeness of her feelings for Mr Emberton. When he was with her, she was sure he was all her heart could desire. When she saw his merry blue eyes and listened to his deep voice, she seemed to be at the threshold of that magical country called love, waiting tremulously for that one long step which would take her across to the land where the days were long and sunny, and where the unicorns played on the crushed pearls of the beach beside the sapphire river.

But when he was gone, she was uncomfortable and had doubts. She longed for the next time she would see him so that these doubts would fade away again.

Then there was that wretched cat. Did she not see Lord Dantrey almost immediately after the cat had run across her path? 'Close the window, Sally,' she said sharply. The candle flames were being blown in the draught and 'winding sheets' were curling about the candles. Sally went to do as she was bid, with her usual nods and winks and grimaces, as if aware of some nasty secret that she could tell if only she would. Lady Godolphin had told Diana that she put up with Sally's peculiar mannerisms because Sally was a genius at her job. But Diana found Sally an uncomfortable person to have around and found herself wishing from time to time that she had Sarah's company.

She kept Mr Emberton's face firmly in her

mind's eye before she fell asleep, hoping to dream of him, but it was Lord Dantrey's lips that bore down on her own and Lord Dantrey's body that made her own burn and ache. She awoke briefly with a cry of distress, turned over and fell asleep, to dream this time of riding out with her father's hunt on a clear autumn day when the bracken shone gold in the clear mellow light and the sharp air was tangy with wood smoke.

Lady Godolphin awoke with a feeling that it would be a very good thing to stay in bed and pull the covers over her head. Arthur, Colonel Brian, had turned unaccountably formal when he had taken his leave. Grimy fog had permeated the room despite the drawn blinds and curtains and closed shutters. No sounds filtered up from the street below, a sure sign that the fog was very thick indeed. Sally came twitching in and drew the curtains, let up the blinds, leaned out and opened the shutters, filling the bedroom with grey light.

'What's the time,' mumbled Lady Godolphin.

'Twelve noon, my lady.'

'Too early to get up,' said Lady Godolphin. 'I did not send for you.'

'Two gentlemen have been waiting below to see you this past hour, my lady.'

'Oh, lor'. Who are they?'

'The Reverend Charles Armitage and Mr Radford.'

'They should know not to come a-calling at this unspeakable hour. Follicles!' grumbled Lady Godolphin. 'I suppose I had better get up. No hope of them taking themselves off anywhere?'

'No, my lady. Matter of the urgentest, that they said, but I said you was not to be awoke, but after they became insistent, Mr Mice said to rouse you.'

'Very well,' groaned Lady Godolphin. 'I do wish Charles Armitage was one of those quiet spiritual kinds of vicars. He always seems to bring drama with him.'

It took an hour for Lady Godolphin to put on her face and what she called her 'negligent' and declare herself fit to see visitors.

'Well, Charles? Mr Radford?' demanded Lady Godolphin as both men rose to meet her. 'What's amiss?'

The vicar and the squire waited until she was seated before the vicar began to speak.

'When did Diana arrive to stay with

134

you?' he demanded.

Lady Godolphin's eyes looked everywhere but at the vicar.

'Don't rightly recall,' she said at last.

'Then we will ask your servants, ma'am.'

'No, don't do that,' said Lady Godolphin wearily. 'I'll tell you what happened . . .'

The two men listened to her, the vicar in mounting fury, and the little squire with increasing distress.

'Well, it's all your own fault, Charles,' said Lady Godolphin when the story of Diana's escapade with Lord Dantrey was finally out. 'You *would* encourage her to dress up as a man. But we may forget about the whole thing, you know. As I told you, I went to see Dantrey himself and he promised he would say nothing of the matter. Diana's still a virago intax. *She* told me herself that there was nothing but a kiss between them and that kiss was only because Dantrey had an understandably low view of her morals. Not only that, seems like some of the old villains like Guy Wentwater were spreading filth about your girls. Dantrey met Wentwater on his travels. So you see, you may as well be comfortable again. Why, if I thought for a moment the girl's reputation was ruined, I would have sent for you express. Diana's been behaving very nicely . . .'

'It's not that, ma'am,' said Squire Radford, straightening his old-fashioned bag wig with a nervous hand. 'Diana must marry this Dantrey. There is nothing else to be done.'

'But *why?*'

'Because Diana had obviously been recognized. Mr Armitage received an anonymous letter.' After the letter had been shown to Lady Godolphin, the squire continued, 'What if the writer of this letter should speak up when the Season is at its height? *Then* everyone would say she had to marry Dantrey.'

'Well, they might say that anyway.'

'But it wouldn't *matter,*' said Squire Radford. 'No one really cares what is said about *married* women. But scandal can destroy the hopes of any young miss.'

'Follicles!' screamed Lady Godolphin in exasperation. 'I used to think Mary Wollstonecraft and her right for women a load of . . . of . . . fustian. But now! Hark'ee, Charles Armitage. Is it not unfair this world of ours? A man may do as he pleases. He may drink and gamble and keep a stable of mistresses and he is accounted no end of an out-and-outer. But a gentlewoman must needs primp and simper and *die* of boredom in order to be comma fault.'

'*Comme il faut,*' said the squire. 'Your nerves are overwrought, dear lady. Your charming sex was made to help and support man and to bear his children. That is God's will and it should not be questioned.'

'It's no use us sitting here argyfying,' said the vicar sourly. 'Fetch Diana down.'

'There's no sense in wrecking the poor girl's life by telling her she's got to be married,' said Lady Godolphin. 'She has behaved shockingly and badly but it's not her fault she was brought up wrong, what with your wife, Charles, living in a comma of cheap quack medicines. And you yourself! 'Tis a wonder your lady did not give birth to a pair of hounds.'

'Diana's got to be told,' said the vicar sternly. 'She's got to learn the folly of her ways.'

'Diana's already learned them,' snapped Lady Godolphin. 'In this short time, she's turned out the sweetest little lady you ever did see. What's more, I have hopes of Mr Emberton asking for her hand in marriage.'

'The new tenant at the Wentwater place?'

said the squire. 'I do not think he has even met her.'

'That's where you're wrong,' said Lady Godolphin triumphantly. 'He followed her to town and he was here, in this very house, for dinner last night, making sheep's eyes at her. She is not indifferent to him, neither.'

'I am sure Mr Emberton is an inestimable young man,' said the squire. 'But what do we really know of him? Parents? Background?'

'Blood line?' put in the vicar.

'I've gone into all that,' said Lady Godolphin, not even realizing in her eagerness to help Diana wed the splendid Mr Emberton that she was lying. 'He's a gentleman born and bred.'

'Then let us hope Diana has not become too fond of him,' sighed the squire. 'For she must marry Lord Dantrey.'

There was a gasp from the doorway and Diana stood there, her eyes wide and dark.

'Papa! You *know?* Oh, Lady Godolphin, I had not thought *you* would betray me.'

'I didn't,' said Lady Godolphin gruffly. 'Someone has sent your Papa an anonymous letter. You were seen with Dantrey in a coffee house and so it seems as if you'll have to marry him.'

'I cannot,' said Diana desperately. 'He *hates* me.'

'Stow it,' said her father rudely. 'You'll do as you're told, miss. Where is Dantrey to be found?'

'At Limmer's,' said Lady Godolphin.

The squire stood up. 'Let us go, Charles, and get this exceedingly unpleasant business over with as soon as possible.'

'Don't. Please don't,' begged Diana.

She clutched at the squire's sleeve. He gently disengaged himself and said firmly, 'I cannot help but feel you have come off extremely lightly in this disgraceful matter, Miss Diana. It is no use begging and pleading. I suggest you pray for forgiveness, if you have not already done so, and think of the trouble and anxiety you have caused . . . you are causing . . . your parents.'

'You are too sakkimonious for my taste,' said Lady Godolphin, putting a pudgy arm around Diana's shoulders. 'Be off with you then. You will not find Dantrey an easy mark. He may think you arranged the whole thing in order to trap him.'

'He will,' wailed Diana, beginning to cry. 'It's happened to him before and he said he wouldn't marry the girl, no matter what anyone said. He despises me already. What will he think now? Oh dear, I left my trunk at Limmer's and I did not pay my bill!'

'Don't matter,' said Lady Godolphin, pulling out a rouge-stained handkerchief and dabbing at Diana's tears. 'We'll have breakfast. Everything looks better after breakfast.'

The vicar turned in the doorway and glared at his drooping daughter. 'You and I will have a talk when I return,' he growled. 'It ain't no use putting the blame on me and trying to make me feel guilty. I DON'T FEEL GUILTY!' And cramming his shovel hat on his head, he left the room with the squire at his heels.

Grey-brown, choking fog engulfed them. The fog was so thick, so dense, that the parish lamps were still lit, feeble flickering lights behind dirty glass globes. In front of shops, the fog turned golden yellow in the light from the windows without allowing any visibility. One found oneself walking through thick golden fog in front of the shops and plunging into dirty grey fog again on the other side of the window.

The vicar and the squire had decided to

walk, since Conduit Street was only a short distance away from Hanover Square. The pillars of St George's Church suddenly loomed up out of the thinning fog on the south side of the square, like the ruined columns of some antique Greek building, since the bulk of the church was veiled in fog.

They pressed themselves against the side of a building as two Irish chairmen came charging along the narrow pavement with their cry of 'Make way!' At the corner of Conduit Street, the vicar threw a crossing sweeper a coin.

The little squire found himself dreading the forthcoming interview, since his sympathies lay with Lord Dantrey. To him it seemed perfectly natural that a gentleman should take advantage of the situation. The squire privately thought that Diana Armitage had behaved like a trollop. The world was full of girls who were delighted with their role in life, which was to flatter and please gentlemen. Why should Miss Diana consider herself different?

At Limmer's, the vicar paid Diana's bill and said he would collect 'Mr Armitage's' trunk after he had seen Lord Dantrey. The squire found himself hoping that Lord Dantrey would be out.

But Lord Dantrey was abovestairs in his room, they were told, and after a short while a servant came back to say his lordship would be pleased to see them.

Lord Dantrey looked anything but pleased. His eyes held a cynical gleam as he sat down opposite the vicar and the squire.

'You are no doubt come,' said Lord Dantrey languidly, 'to coerce me into marriage with your daughter. I have behaved stupidly, that I admit. Had I my wits about me, then I should have been alive to the situation.'

'The fact is,' said the vicar, keeping his volatile temper on a tight rein, 'that I have had this here anonymous letter. Were it simply a matter of you keeping quiet and Diana keeping quiet, then it would not matter. I have no desire to see a daughter of mine ruined . . .'

'Then you should take better care of her.'

'. . . *ruined* by a man who already carries the reputation of a rake.'

'Now, dear vicar,' said Lord Dantrey gently, 'you would not have me call you out.'

'I'm only stating the facts,' said the vicar. 'Seems you knew she was a girl from the start. Why did you encourage her in this ploy?'

'I was bored, she interested me . . . only briefly, alas. My taste does not run to hoydens.'

'Then you must marry her. An you do not,' said the vicar, leaning forward and clenching his plump fists on his knees, 'your reputation will be mud.'

'You forget. I am accustomed to that. I have no intention of marrying your daughter. I do not like her.'

'Sir!' cried the squire, outraged, all his sympathies now with the absent Diana.

'Furthermore,' went on Lord Dantrey as if the squire had not spoken, 'no one else seemed to take her for a woman except myself. As a matter of fact, she was even pressganged on Tower Hill.'

'Oh, merciful God!' cried the little vicar, wondering if there were any more horrors that Lady Godolphin had neglected to tell him. 'I have done nothing to deserve this. Oh, sharper than a serpent's tooth, it is to have a thankless child. St Luke, chapter . . .'

'Shakespeare. King Lear.'

'What! '

'Not the bible. Shakespeare,' said Lord Dantrey. 'And if you wonder what you have done to deserve this, I think you have more good fortune than you deserve. You allow your daughter to dress as a man when she ought to be learning the arts of ladylike accomplishment. You then try to force her on me in marriage when there is no reason to do so that I can see, unless you wish to get your hands on my fortune.'

The vicar choked and spluttered with rage.

'Sir,' said the squire, looking at Lord Dantrey with dislike. 'You forget about the anonymous letter. You forget that, knowing Diana Armitage to be a lady, you nonetheless allowed yourself to be seen about with her, and you even thrust your attentions upon her.'

'Miss Diana was extremely fortunate,' said Lord Dantrey sharply. 'I treated her to an excess of civility, nothing more. Very well, gentlemen, I admit I behaved badly. But marry Miss Diana Armitage, I most certainly will not. What exactly did the letter say?'

The vicar produced the much-fingered anonymous letter and handed it over.

Lord Dantrey took out his quizzing glass,

144

polished it, and studied the letter. 'Hubbold's coffee house,' he mused. 'Now let me think . . .'

The vicar opened his mouth to say something, but the squire restrained him with a warning look.

'The only thing I did notice,' said Lord Dantrey slowly, 'was the presence of two very young men, more schoolboys than men. The light was bad in the coffee house, but it did strike me that they bore a strong resemblance to Miss Diana Armitage.'

'Peregrine and James!' said the squire.

'Can't be,' said the vicar. 'They're at Eton. And why would they send their father an anonymous letter?'

'Because they did not want papa to know they were not at school when they should have been,' said Lord Dantrey, swinging his quizzing glass to and fro on its long silk cord.

'We'd best go to Eton and find out,' said the squire eagerly. 'You do not want this man as a son-in-law, Charles, if it can possibly be helped.'

'No, I grant you that,' said the vicar. 'Took a dislike to him as soon as I set eyes on him.'

'If you will forgive me taking exception to your discussing me as if I were not here,' said Lord Dantrey silkily, 'I should like, for my part, to emphasize that nothing on this earth could persuade me, after meeting you, my very dear reverend, to ally my name with that of your family.'

'We'll see about that,' said the vicar. 'After we get back from Eton.'

Diana and Lady Godolphin waited nervously for the return of the vicar and the squire. But the hours grew longer and the day darker and still they did not return. They discussed the problem earnestly. Lady Godolphin grew more prepared to look on the bright side, saying that Lord Dantrey was quite a good catch, while Diana became more and more vehement in her protestations that Lord Dantrey was unfeeling and evil.

Colonel Brian had promised to call to escort Lady Godolphin and Diana to the play. Lady Godolphin had not asked Mr Emberton to join the party, feeling that a little absence might make the heart grow fonder, but when he called late that afternoon to thank her for dinner and to pay his respects to Diana, she abruptly invited him to accompany them that evening. If Diana were to marry a man she did not like, then let her at least have one evening in the company of a man she did.

When the two ladies went upstairs to prepare for the evening, Lady Godolphin consoled Diana by pointing out that if the vicar had had any success with Lord Dantrey, he would have returned immediately. It would be just like him, said Lady Godolphin acidly, to return to the country and sulk if he did not get his own way.

Mr Emberton kept looking thoughtfully at Diana's set face, revealed in the light of the carriage lamps as the chariot bearing them to the playhouse lurched and inched its way through the suffocating fog.

Diana was wearing an evening gown richly ornamented *à la militaire*, gold braid and netted buttons forming a sort of epaulette on each shoulder. Her hair was carefully arranged in dishevelled curls and crowned with laurel leaves.

Lady Godolphin was wearing a pink merino gown with white silk stripes, and on her head she sported a pink gauze turban.

Her face was so thickly enamelled that when she smiled, little cracks appeared in the paint at the corners of her mouth and eyes.

The play was called *The Beau in Love,* a light piece of nonsense, greatly appreciated by the audience. It was different from Diana's last visit to the theatre. This time she was seated in a box, above the hurly-burly of the pit, and since the production was popular, she could actually hear most of what was said on the stage.

For a little while she was able to lose herself in the play. But as it neared its end she looked across the theatre and saw Lord Dantrey. He was sitting in a box opposite with his friend, Mr Fane. As she looked, he raised his quizzing glass and she quickly dropped her eyes, her heart beating hard.

Lord Dantrey lowered his glass. He had not at first been sure that the modish beauty in the opposite box was Diana Armitage. Somehow he kept expecting to see the 'boy' Diana, but the elegant creature sitting beside Lady Godolphin could never in a hundred years be mistaken for a man. Perhaps he was wrong. If it were Diana, then this was a Diana a hundred times more beautiful than the one he had seen in the park. Bands of fog lay across the theatre, distorting vision. Of course it must be she. It could not be anyone else with that Emberton fellow, not to mention the extraordinary Lady Godolphin. He had a sudden desire to talk to her again, to warn her about Mr Emberton. But that might be taken as a sign that he wished to marry the girl. He was now sure the vicar and Diana knew exactly what they were about. Diana had not lost her way hunting. She had deliberately called at his door.

But if she wanted to compromise herself to get your hand in marriage, said a niggling voice in his brain, would it not have been better to stay the night and then have her father call in the morning? He shook his head to clear it. As he watched, Jack Emberton bent his head and said something to Diana and she looked up at him and smiled. All at once Lord Dantrey found himself becoming very angry indeed. She had no right to smile like that. In fact, he would tell her so himself.

'What ails you?' asked his friend, Mr Tony Fane, at his elbow. 'You look as black as thunder.'

'Nothing,' said Lord Dantrey, rallying. 'The play is not to my taste.'

'Indeed?' said Mr Fane. 'I did not notice you paying much attention to the play. Your eyes have been fixed on Miss Diana Armitage for this age.'

'Nonsense! Can't see anything in this curst fog, Tony. The whole of London is turning black with the exception of yourself. You are changing to a ripe mahogany colour.'

Mr Fane had browned his face and the backs of his hands with walnut as was the fashion, but he had applied it with too liberal a hand, and had already been mistaken for the Jamaican actor, Romeo Coates, by a crowd of sightseers outside the playhouse.

Mr Fane was large, fat and jovial. He was younger than Lord Dantrey. The pair had met two years before when Lord Dantrey's travels had taken him to Greece. Mr Fane had been making the Grand Tour and was delighted to meet another Englishman. Since then, they had written to each other and Lord Dantrey's return to England had found Mr Fane eager to renew the friendship. Lord Dantrey sometimes envied his friend his enjoyment of life and easy, undemanding good nature. Lord Dantrey was still concerned about putting the Osbadiston estates in good order, since he had a long lease on the lands and property. His father, the Earl of Juxborough, would brook no interference in his own estates and was content to supply his eldest son with as much money as he wanted, provided he played farmer elsewhere. Mr Fane, on the other hand, was a true gentleman of his times and found a life of pleasure and idleness suited him very well. He sometimes was amazed that Lord Dantrey should wish to boggle his mind with crop rotation and fertilizers, but he was too idle to interfere in anyone else's mode of life.

Lord Dantrey was debating whether or not to wait for the farce which followed the play when he noticed Lady Godolphin's party getting to its feet.

'Let us go,' he said abruptly. Mr Fane looked meaningfully in the direction of Lady Godolphin's box but did not say anything.

Lord Dantrey fairly hustled him along, through the crush of fashionably dressed people, brushing off the clawing hands of the prostitutes who were offering their wares for two shillings and a glass of rum.

Prices had gone up, even in whoring,

reflected Mr Fane with mild astonishment. Not so long ago it had been only one shilling and a glass of rum that was demanded.

He and Lord Dantrey came face to face with Lady Godolphin's party at the foot of the stairs. Diana looked full at Lord Dantrey, coloured and lowered her eyes, her thick lashes fanning out over her cheeks. Her military-style gown had been cleverly cut to show the rich fullness of her bosom to advantage. Her face looked thinner and yet softer. He had somehow thought of her as having a strong masculine chin, but there was nothing at all masculine about the beautiful girl who stood before him, desperately trying to avoid his gaze.

Just then a party of roistering bucks and bloods thrust their way in front of Lord Dantrey, blocking Diana from view.

An elderly gentleman on the other side of Mr Fane objected loudly to their behaviour and started hitting out with his stick. Someone else punched the leading buck and soon the theatre was in an uproar of shrieking, fainting women and cursing men. By the time order was restored and Lord Dantrey was able to look around, Diana, Lady Godolphin, Mr Emberton and Colonel

Brian were already on the road to Hanover Square.

Mr Emberton was invited in to share the tea tray at Lady Godolphin's. But, as she was about to lead her little party into the Yellow Saloon, Lady Godolphin found her arm caught by Colonel Brian. 'I crave a word with you in private, dear lady,' he whispered.

Lady Godolphin cast an anguished look at Diana. She felt she should not leave the girl unchaperoned. On the other hand, she felt she might die of curiosity if she did not find out as soon as possible what Colonel Brian had to say. Lady Godolphin thought quickly. If she ordered tea and asked for the fire to be made up, then there would be servants coming and going. She would leave the door of the Yellow Room open.

And so Diana found herself alone with Mr Jack Emberton. She sat silently on a sofa in front of the fire, playing with the sticks of her fan.

He sat down beside her and studied her averted face.

'Who was that man?' he asked abruptly.

'What man?' Diana's voice was low, almost a whisper. A log shifted in the grate and sent up a spurt of smoky flame. Fog veiled the room, giving a tapestry effect to the furniture and pictures.

'You know. He was in the park. And he looked at you in the theatre.'

'Dantrey,' said Diana wearily. 'Lord Dantrey.' She added bitterly, 'I thought you knew everyone in London.'

'Ah, *Dantrey*,' said Mr Emberton. 'Of course I know him. That is why I asked you his name—because his face looked so familiar.'

All at once, Diana found herself engulfed by a great wave of terror. She was sure that as soon as her father returned she would be forced to marry Lord Dantrey, hell-bent on meting out a life of punishment. Her hopes that Lord Dantrey would deal with her father as he had dealt with Miss Blessingham's parents had quite gone. Diana could not imagine anyone standing up to her father. Despite her fear, she found it almost strange that she no longer regretted being a woman. Men were not forced into marriage, she thought naively, forgetting all the younger sons pressed to marry heiresses they did not like. But her escapade with Lord Dantrey had cured her of any longings in that direction. The only advantage in being a man that she could now think of was that one could hurt without fear of censure.

Mr Emberton sat beside her, solid and reliable. Suddenly Diana could not bear him to learn of her forthcoming marriage without offering him an explanation. Her real motive was a desire to unburden herself, combined with an aching need for help.

'Mr Emberton,' she said. 'I am in very bad trouble and it concerns Lord Dantrey. I must tell someone. I must tell someone who will never speak of it. Can I trust you?'

He put his hand to his heart, his blue eyes serious. 'I would die rather than breathe a word of anything you may tell me, Miss Diana. I would die for you.'

Was there a *staginess* about his statement, about his voice? But Diana hesitated for only a moment and then plunged into her tale. She told him everything, including the gypsy's prediction, although she changed 'lover' to 'gentleman'.

Mr Emberton listened carefully and wondered how to turn it to his advantage. Although his friend, Mr Peter Flanders, had accused him of blackmail, Mr Emberton did not care to use that method. His original plan of getting Diana to fall in love with him and then getting the vicar to pay him off was by far the more attractive course. That way, he would come out of it rich, and apparently the injured party, and with his reputation intact. Any open, criminal threat could injure his future at the card tables. Furthermore, there had been a quiet air of menace about Lord Dantrey which made him nervous. Unlike Lord Dantrey, he considered *all* women to have loose morals. Some were only better at disguising the fact than Diana. His brief amorous adventures had been with the lower stratum of the Fashionable Impure, or with gullible young matrons looking for a release from marital boredom. Being *in* society but not *of* society, Mr Emberton considered the ton, both male and female, to be mostly eccentric. He was unmoved by Diana's humiliation at Lord Dantrey's hands. In fact, looking furtively sideways at Diana's deep bosom, trim waist and neat ankles, he could only wonder that his lordship had shown such restraint.

He finally grasped that, although Diana considered the marriage inevitable, no decision had been reached and the vicar was still absent.

He prided himself on being a man of action and, as soon as he finally decided on a way to turn the affair to his advantage, he wasted no time.

'So I do not know what to do, Mr Emberton,' Diana was saying.

He seized her hands. 'Let us elope . . . Diana!'

'I could not. Oh, Mr Emberton, I would not have you marry me simply to save me from Lord Dantrey.' In a burst of gratitude, Diana picked up a cup of tea and held it out to him, the first thing she could think of to give him to thank him.

Unfortunately, that was the precise moment that Mr Emberton decided to take Diana in his arms and the tea went down his waistcoat.

'I am sorry,' babbled Diana miserably, jumping to her feet and oversetting the silver bowl of sugar loaves which went scattering across the carpet into the foggy shadows in the corners of the room.

'Diana,' said Lady Godolphin, coming in, much flushed. 'You *are* a clumsy girl.'

One of Lady Godolphin's well-trained footmen materialized with a dustpan and brush and began to clean up the mess.

'Where is Colonel Brian?' asked Diana, shaken by Mr Emberton's proposal and upset by her own clumsiness, which she thought she had left behind with her masculine clothes.

'Gone,' said Lady Godolphin lugubriously. 'I shall never understand men.'

She sat down and the three talked in a desultory way, each wrapped in their own thoughts. Mr Emberton was wondering how he could get Diana alone again so that he could persuade her to elope. Of course he didn't plan to marry the girl. He would drive north in the direction of Gretna Green as slowly as possible and make sure the letter he left for Mr Armitage would have the desired effect. With any luck, they would be stopped as early in the journey as Barnet. That way, it would save him expensive tolls and, provided they were stopped before they had racked up for the night, then the vicar would be reassured that Diana was still a virgin and would therefore be eager to pay Mr Emberton to go away.

In order for the plan to work he would need to get her away by tomorrow morning, before the vicar returned.

Diana was turning his idea of elopement

over and over in her brain. And the more she thought about it, the more attractive it seemed. Oh, to be able to run away from the whole horrid mess and disgrace. A wave of self-pity engulfed her. Frederica, the only one who might care, was at school. Her other sisters were happily and *respectably* married. Her father cared for nothing but the hunt, thought Diana miserably, forgetting that only a short time ago she had thought of little else herself. Mama was kind and loving any time she managed to surface from her twilight world of drugs and concoctions, but had never been the sort of mother a daughter would run to in time of trouble.

Lady Godolphin discoursed on the weather (terrible), the absurd fashion for white bread (full of chalk), and the state of the nation (unspeakable), while inside her mind she was fretting over her recent conversation with Colonel Brian. Instead of suggesting he should join her in her bedchamber as she fully expected, he had talked long and mournfully of his increasing years and his desire to reform his life before his place in Heaven was given up to somebody else. In vain had Lady Godolphin suggested he take rhubarb pills to clear his system, in vain had she cried that an upset stomach always led to gloom and despondency; it seemed the colonel was determined to spend a good, decent and blameless life and that Lady Godolphin was not going to be part of it.

At last Mr Emberton rose to take his leave. There was no chance for even a brief word in private with Diana.

He walked to his lodgings where his friend, Peter Flanders, was waiting for him, and lost no time in recounting the adventures of Diana Armitage.

'Don't tangle with Dantrey,' said Mr Flanders, winding his long limbs around his chair leg. 'A hard man to cross, I've heard.'

'If I could get the girl to elope with me in the morning, then I would not need to cross swords with Dantrey,' snapped Mr Emberton, 'but that over-painted tart, Lady Godolphin, came in before I could really begin to persuade her. If only there was some way . . .'

'Send her a note,' said Mr Flanders.

'What?'

'I said, send her a note. You're always so devious. Simplest way is best. Write out something and we'll both walk round to Hanover Square and deliver it. Simply tell her you'll wait at the far corner of the square at about seven. Can't make it earlier or you might not wake up. Once you're off, I'll call on the Reverend and tip him off. Gone away, has he? He'll be back some time tomorrow so, to slow things up, stage a breakdown before you even get out of London.'

Mr Emberton looked at his thin friend with reluctant admiration. 'By George, I'll do it!' he said. 'Where's pen and paper?'

Soon he was bent over his desk, breathing heavily as he laboriously penned the words, pausing every few minutes to consult Dr Johnson's dictionary.

At last he was well satisfied. 'It will mean rousing the servants,' he said, sanding the letter, 'and that butler might tell Lady Godolphin.'

'Need to take a risk,' said Mr Flanders cheerfully. 'All's fair in love and war.'

He repeated, 'All's fair in love and war,' nodding his head wisely, too pleased with the neatness of the phrase to consider that Mr Emberton was not at war and never likely to expose his person to such a danger. Nor was he in love.

Mr Tony Fane shifted uneasily in his chair. Watier's, that club at the corner of Bolton Street famed for its cuisine, gambling and suicides, was thin of company, due no doubt to the thickness of the fog outside.

Mr Fane was meditating miserably on the vagaries of male fashion while sharing a bowl of Rumfustian—a punch composed of twelve eggs whisked, a quart of strong beer, a pint of gin, a bottle of sherry, and nutmeg, sugar and lemon rind—with Lord Dantrey, Mr Harvey-Maxwell, a dreamy poet, and that old war horse, Lord Saunders.

Pantaloons, mused Mr Fane, had been quite comfortable when they had become high fashion not so very long ago. They were tights, reaching down to where the calf narrows into the ankle and buttoned there over a neat expanse of striped silk stocking. Their sides were braided in semi-military fashion. Top boots were worn with breeches, but hessian boots or shoes with pantaloons. So far so good. But *then* fickle fashion had decreed that a gentleman should put on his pantaloons when they were still damp and let them dry on his body in order to render them skin tight. How did the rest fare, thought Mr Fane, as the conversation about him rose and fell. For his part, the insides of his plump thighs were already rubbed raw, what with the damp inside and the cold outside, and the excellent dinner he had just enjoyed was straining at the seams as if grouse, pheasant, quail and venison fought to escape and return to their natural habitat. His black waistcoat, embroidered with gold flowers, no longer lay over his stomach in a smooth line but in a series of hard ridges.

His attention turned to his friend, Lord Dantrey. Dantrey was leaning back in his chair, his odd green and gold eyes under their heavy lids looking amused at something Mr Harvey-Maxwell was saying. But there was something about that Armitage girl that upset Dantrey badly, reflected Mr Fane.

With a great effort, Mr Fane forced himself to listen to the conversation. Mr Harvey-Maxwell was hailing all females as divine creatures 'without whom us men would be boorish, savage brutes."

'Perhaps the female of the species is not as weak and feminine as she would like to appear,' said Lord Dantrey.

'I don't think the fair creatures enjoy playing the part of helpless innocents,' said Lord Saunders. 'I'm not just talking about the ones in society. I remember my great-grandfather who was in Marlborough's campaign telling me that a great number of women disguised themselves as men and enlisted in the military.'

'I can hardly believe that,' said Mr Fane, his interest aroused. 'Surely they must have been discovered easily.'

'Not a bit of it,' said Lord Saunders. 'One woman got forty lashes in the navy and even then she was not discovered. It was only when she had to be stripped off completely after receiving a wound that the matter came out. The men they were sharing quarters with never discovered these women's secret either. Most of them drank and swore like troopers.'

'Then if it was such a great secret,' said Lord Dantrey, 'how did they guess there were so many enlisted women?'

'Oh, because once these Amazons had enough prize money, once they were getting older, they left the military and set up a shop or something and reverted to their former female status.'

'Why do they do it?' asked Lord Dantrey with increasing interest. 'Why should any woman want to be a man?'

'Freedom,' said Lord Saunders. 'Aye, you may stare. But in my day we spoke more open on such matters, and in my father's day, even society women swore something awful. They do it to get away from the tyranny of babies, seduction, more babies and, in the lower orders, poor servants' wages and horrible servants' conditions. Look at all the Penelopes and Clarissas getting ready for the next Season. They are told they must catch a man and most of them are happy with that idea. But *after* they catch their man, what then? They never see us. We're either in our clubs or on the hunting field.'

'Any woman I loved,' said Mr Harvey-Maxwell, 'I would worship until death. I would sit with her in the evenings and . . .'

'Card her wool,' said Lord Saunders with a great horse laugh. 'Nonsense. Fellow like you would worship your wife up till the first two brats and then you would attach yourself to some other reigning belle and sigh at *her* feet.'

'But these women—the ones who enlisted —would be expected to fight,' exclaimed Mr Fane. 'I can just imagine the dears throwing away their guns and shrieking like the blue devil.'

'It is said a lot were braver than the men,' laughed Lord Saunders. 'Here! I'll tell you a *real* story from my great-grandfather's time about a woman called Christian Cavenaugh. Whether she was christened Christina, no one will ever know. Anyway, Christian lodged with an aunt who kept a public house in Dublin. On her aunt's death, she married the waiter and had by him three children. He was kidnapped and carried off to Holland and pressed into the army. When Christian heard what had happened, she placed her children under the care of her brother, dressed herself as a man, enlisted as a private soldier, and went out in search of her husband.

'She fought in the battle of Landen where she got a wound in the ankle, and then she was made prisoner by the French. When there was an exchange of prisoners between the French and the English, she was able to return home. On her return, she quarrelled with a sergeant in her regiment over a girl. A duel followed in which she wounded her antagonist. After this, her relations were able to get her a discharge to escape the consequences of this encounter. She then, however, enlisted in another regiment. At Donauwath she received a bullet in the hip, but still managed to escape discovery.

'After the battle of Hochstadt, she found her husband, who was making love to a Dutchwoman. Christian was much altered in appearance by this time but she told her husband who she was and reproached him with his infidelity, nevertheless pointing out that he must not think of her as his wife until the end of the war.

'She went through the Battle of Ramillies and had her skull fractured, in the treatment of which she had her sex discovered, since they stripped her off when she was unconscious.

'She was then allowed to join her husband and was permitted, first, to cook for the regiment, and afterwards to become sutler. Her husband was shortly afterwards killed in battle, and a few weeks later she found consolation with another husband, Hugh Jones, a grenadier. She was now an official marauder as well as sutler, and ranged over the field of battle after very encounter, searching and stripping the dead. At one of the many sieges she lost her second husband.

'She then returned to England and presented a petition to Queen Anne, setting forth that she had served in the Earl of Orkney's regiment for twelve years, had received several wounds, and had lost two husbands in the service. The Queen gave her a bounty of fifty pounds and a pension of one shilling a day. She went to Dublin, set up a pieshop and married a third time, again a soldier. Once more she joined the barracks as sutler, and so continued until her husband was admitted to Chelsea Hospital, where she lived with him until his death in 1793. She was buried in Chelsea Hospital with full military honours.

'So fill up your glasses and let's have a toast. Gentlemen! I give you Christian Cavenaugh.'

They all drank. Mr Harvey-Maxwell said dreamily it was the most romantic story he had ever heard. Mr Fane shuddered and said Miss Cavenaugh sounded as tough as old boots and all he could think of was her ranging the battlefields, stripping the dead. Lord Dantrey was silent. He was thinking with some surprise that he had never really before considered women as anything but an amusement. He did not know if he quite liked the idea of them having courage and brains. Of course, there were plenty of blue stockings around, but one always assumed they were *pretending* to be clever. But it seemed that Diana Armitage was not unique and her behaviour did not reflect low morals but only a desire for freedom. Strange! He found himself becoming ashamed of his own behaviour, and that annoyed him so much that he called for another bowl of punch and suggested a game of hazard.

Mr Fane managed to forget his fashionable discomforts in the excitement of the play until about five in the morning, when he at last declared himself too sleepy to continue any longer. Mr Harvey-Maxwell said he felt wilted like a flower and opted to leave with Mr Fane. Neither Lord Dantrey nor old Lord Saunders seemed tired and so they were left to their game.

At last, just before seven, they too rose from the tables, Lord Saunders declaring it was an excellent evening, since he had managed to win a fair sum from Lord Dantrey, that gentleman's mind being more on Miss Diana Armitage than it was on the dice.

Lord Dantrey made his way through the

foggy, deserted streets. He walked down Bolton Street, through Berkeley Square, up Bruton Street to Bond Street, and somehow he found himself in the foggy precincts of Hanover Square before he quite realized where he was going.

He leaned against the low railings of the square and studied what he could see of the front of Lady Godolphin's mansion. The large diamond in his stock winked in the flickering light of the parish lamp, and the crystal and gold buttons on his coat glowed against the sombre cloth.

Diana Armitage, he thought gloomily. I do not want a Diana Armitage in my life. I want a soft, feminine, pliable lady who will think I am God.

He laughed at his own arrogance and was about to turn in the direction of his lodgings when he stopped. The door of Lady Godolphin's house was slowly opening.

The fog, which had thinned a little, closed down again.

Lord Dantrey moved forward.

A female figure, heavily veiled, emerged carrying two large bandboxes and quietly closed the door behind her.

Diana!

Now what was she up to?

He drew back a little as Diana looked cautiously to left and right.

She moved down the steps and started to make her way around the square. He hurried after, walking lightly, his evening pumps making no sound on the cobbles. On the other side of the square the black block of a travelling carriage loomed up out of the fog.

All at once Lord Dantrey decided that Miss Diana Armitage was eloping.

He took several brisk steps forward and seized her by the arm.

She let out a squeak and dropped the bandboxes, which rolled away and landed up against the railings.

Diana Armitage looked up into the mocking eyes of Lord Mark Dantrey and wished she were dead.

CHAPTER SIX

'Let me go!' whispered Diana fiercely.

'No. I am persuaded you are eloping.'

'What business is it of yours?'

'It is the business of any gentleman to see that a lady does not make a fool of herself. You are eloping with Mr Emberton.'

'I love him!'

Too much punch, thought Lord Dantrey, as he felt a stabbing pain somewhere in his insides.

'Does he love you?'

'Of course he loves me.'

'Then why elope?'

'Because if I do not,' said Diana in a venomous whisper, 'I shall be forced to marry *you!*'

'How can that be when I most certainly do not want to marry you. Tell your Mr Emberton *that,* and suggest he courts you in the normal manner. Think of your family and do not be so selfish.'

'Papa has not returned. He has not told me what passed between you.'

'He tried to constrain me to marry you because of a certain anonymous letter which reported you were seen with me at Hubbold's coffee house. I reported that I had noticed a couple of young men in the coffee house who bore a marked resemblance to you, although I did not think much about it at the time. Your father thought your twin brothers might have been playing truant from school and, not wishing to be found out in their escapade, settled for sending an anonymous letter. He has gone to Eton. If this proves to be the case, your father will not say any more about the matter. I trust you were not foolish enough to tell Mr Emberton of your escapade?'

'No,' lied Diana, not quite knowing why she was lying.

Mr Peter Flanders walked softly up to the travelling carriage. 'Dantrey's caught her,' he whispered to Jack Emberton.

Mr Emberton swore fluently. 'I have no mind to be called out by Dantrey,' he said at last. 'I shall beat a strategic retreat and find ways to deal with the situation later.'

'Good,' said Mr Flanders, climbing into

the carriage. 'Tell that ox of a coachman to drive on. I had no desire to find myself acting as your second.'

As Diana ran towards the carriage through the fog, she heard the rumble of departing wheels. Unwilling to believe that Mr Emberton had deserted her, she ran around the square, searching this way and that. At last she returned to where Lord Dantrey was standing.

'Gone away?' he enquired pleasantly. He pulled Diana into his arms and held her firmly against him. 'Miss Diana,' he said, 'I urge you not to flaunt the laws of society. It will cause nothing but grief.'

'I am tired of your familiarities, sir,' said Diana between her teeth. 'Let me go.'

'No, you will listen to me first.'

'Listen to you? You fop, you dilettante, you *rake!*'

She wriggled furiously against him. He felt her breasts pushing against his chest, he smelled the clean scent of soap and rose water from her hair, and he gave a little sigh and, holding her even more firmly, bent his mouth to her own. Diana went rigid with shock. He kissed her very gently and sweetly, his mouth pressing gradually deeper and deeper, feeling a great surge of burning desire welling up in him. The desire became so all-consuming, such sweetness shot through with pain, that when he finally freed his mouth and looked down at the stark, white-faced disgust on her face, he could hardly believe the tremendous longing and passion had all been on his side, and he let his arms drop.

Diana raised her hand to slap his face, but he stood looking down at her with an odd intent expression in his eyes. Moving very stiffly, she picked up her bandboxes and stalked like an angry cat towards the door of Lady Godolphin's house.

Lord Dantrey stayed where he was, watching her until she had disappeared. He felt confused and not a little alarmed at the intensity of his feelings. He decided he would be better off avoiding Miss Diana Armitage in the future.

Diana returned to her bed and slept badly. She was eventually awakened by her father who gave her the glad tidings that Peregrine and James had been the authors of the anonymous letter. Everyone was sworn to silence and so she had nothing more to worry about. He was about to deliver himself of a blistering lecture on the folly of her behaviour when Diana burst into tears. She sobbed that she was crying with relief, but she looked so distressed, so agonized, that the vicar decided to beat a hasty retreat.

The vicar had a long talk with Lady Godolphin before removing himself to the country. He questioned her closely about Mr Emberton. In truth, the vicar was more prepared to be indulgent when it came to Diana than he was in the affairs of any of his other children. He had enjoyed Diana's company on the hunting field and at times had been able to forget she was a girl. Lady Godolphin was able to reassure him that Diana was turning out to be a quiet and modish lady and showed none of the awkwardness or gaucherie of which the vicar had complained. Certainly she had upset a tea tray, but that was only on one occasion, and she showed no disposition to be rude in company.

The Reverend Charles Armitage therefore left with Squire Radford for the country, easy in his conscience. It was not usual for the vicar to feel so comfortable within himself and the more comfortable he felt, the more sanctimonious he grew, until the squire found himself relieved when the squat tower of St Charles and St Jude rose above the winter trees. The squire said he would pay his compliments to Mrs Armitage and then go home and go to bed.

The vicarage seemed unnaturally quiet, and it took some ringing of the parlour bell to bring Sarah.

'Where's your mistress?' demanded the vicar, running an appreciative eye over Sarah's trim form.

'In her bed, sir,' replied Sarah with that characteristic toss of her head which sent the ribbons of her cap flying.

'Be so good as to rouse her and tell her that Mr Radford wishes to pay his respects. And before you do that, fetch the brandy.'

The squire shivered a little and edged his chair nearer the fire.

A light sprinkling of snow had fallen, turning the garden outside white and bleak. Great ragged clouds sailed above the bare branches of the trees and a starling piped dismally from the branch of an oak. The vicarage gate had been left unlatched and it swung on its iron hinges, emitting a dreary shriek. Sarah deposited a tray with the brandy bottle and two glasses in front of the gentlemen and then could be heard mounting the stairs to the bedchambers.

'Perhaps I should call later,' said the squire. 'Mrs Armitage is perhaps asleep.'

'Mrs Armitage is always asleep,' growled the vicar. 'She went into Hopeminster last week and you know what *that* means.'

The squire nodded. Mrs Armitage always came back from Hopeminster with a great stock of patent medicines with which she proceeded to dose herself.

The wind gave a great howl about the building and swept away across the bare winter fields.

'The banshee,' shuddered the little squire. 'The Irish would say that was the banshee.'

'And what's a banshee when it's at home?'

The squire sipped his brandy. 'No matter,' he said at last. 'An old, primitive superstition.'

'Do you think this Emberton fellow will do for Diana?'

'I do not know,' said the squire cautiously. 'He seems well enough in his way. Yet, I confess, I feel there is something brutal about him, something that is not quite the gentleman.'

'Being a brute don't mean he ain't a gentleman,' said the vicar. 'London's full o' fashionable brutes. If they ain't brutes, they're tipping about on high heels with their faces full o' paint and not enough in their breeches to . . .'

'Charles!'

'Ah, well, we'll see how this Emberton turns out. Pity about Dantrey. Emberton's more to my taste, but everyone knows Dantrey's worth thousands. Still, I don't want my Diana wed to a rake. They *never* change.'

'My dear Charles, no one could say *you* have spent a celibate life.'

'They couldn't now, could they? Been married for years.'

'That was not what I meant,' said the squire primly. 'There was Jessie last year, and then there was the serving wench over in Hopeminster . . .'

'Here!' said the vicar. 'What if Mrs Armitage should hear you! Fie, for shame.'

'I'm cold,' sighed the squire. 'I did not mean to start to read you a lecture. Where is Mr Pettifor these days?'

'In church, where he always is,' said the vicar. Mr Pettifor was the vicar's overworked curate.

'You are very lucky, Charles,' said the squire, 'to have such a willing and able young man as Mr Pettifor. When one considers your many absences . . .'

'Jimmy! Faith, 'tis not like you. First you attack me on my lack of morals and then on my lack of religion. Where's that girl? What can be keeping her?'

Just then the door opened and Sarah came in, all her normal cockiness fled. 'Oh, Mr Armitage,' she said. 'Mistress is not in her room. Mrs Hammer says she come downstairs, looking fair mazed, about a couple of hours ago, and the next thing she hears the door bang. Mrs Hammer had something boiling on the stove so she couldn't go see. Mrs Armitage don't seem to have taken no mantle nor wrap and her was wearing one of her muslins.'

Both men turned and stared out of the window where tiny flakes of snow were beginning to fall.

'Get John Summer,' said the vicar. 'Get the lads from the village. I'll need to go out, Jimmy. One of them concoctions has finally twisted her brain.'

'I'll come with you,' said the squire quietly. 'We must ask if anyone has seen her.'

The curate, Mr Pettifor, walked into the room, his long nose red with cold. 'Where's Mrs Armitage?' asked the vicar. 'Seems she's wandered out.'

'I saw a lady in a thin gown walking across the fields in the direction of Saxon Mere,' said Mr Pettifor. 'She was staggering as she walked and so I thought I would go after her as soon as my duties were finished.'

'Come with us now,' said the vicar. 'Please God, she hasn't done anything silly.'

They hurried out into the bleak, grey iciness of the day. Ice crackled under their feet as they made their way through the churchyard and out over the fields. Mr Pettifor showed a desire to chatter and looked disappointed when the vicar snarled at him to be quiet. Poor Mr Pettifor, thought the squire. What a lonely life he must lead. No one ever seemed to want to spend much time in his company.

It was only when the livid mirror of Saxon Mere appeared at the bottom of a long slope that the squire felt a sickening sense of dread. He had, up till then, fully expected to see Mrs Armitage weaving her way across the fields, totally under the influence of some patent medicine. The landscape looked so grim, so empty. They were moving through the still heart of winter, where memories of summers past were lost and hope of summers to come not yet born.

It seemed almost inevitable when the vicar said in a strangely flat voice, 'There's something floating out there. Pettifor, the boat!'

The squire began to pray silently, over and over again.

Mr Pettifor fumbled with the oars and the vicar gave an oath and told him to sit in the stern. He would row himself. The boat crackled through the thin ice at the water's edge. Frozen reeds stood sentinel, tall reeds, momentarily barring the view. Then the boat moved out into the lake as little hard pellets of snow struck their faces and began to erase the far landscape.

The wind rose and little angry waves smacked and sucked at the sides of the boat. The thing in the lake for which they were headed danced tantalizingly, always seeming to be just a little in front of them.

Then the wind stopped as abruptly as it had risen. The vicar shipped the oars and leaned over the side of the boat. Everything was very silent, as if the countryside was waiting.

The vicar of St Charles and St Jude looked down into the dead face of his wife. Weeds had trapped her floating body. She had a faint smile on her face and her sightless eyes looked straight up to the empty grey bowl of the sky.

'Get her aboard,' said the vicar.

Sobbing with shock, the curate wrestled and heaved until the sodden body was pulled over the side.

The vicar picked up the oars and rowed as hard as he could to the shore.

'Get out,' he snapped. 'I'll carry her myself.'

He lifted his wife in his arms and stepped out onto the shore. Then he turned his eyes up to Heaven and shouted, 'I didn't like her! Do You hear? *I didn't like her one bit.*' And with great sobs racking his body he heaved the corpse of his wife over his shoulder and set off across the fields with the squire and the curate stumbling behind.

They were all gathered at the graveside in the bitter cold to say goodbye to their mother—all the beautiful Armitage girls.

Minerva, tall and rather stern in her grief, Annabelle, golden-haired and modish, Deirdre, red-haired, her face made sharp and thin with misery, stately Daphne without a black hair out of place, but with her great eyes shadowed with loss, Diana holding little Frederica to her side. The twins, Peregrine and James, stood with the Armitage girls' husbands.

The vicar's brother, Sir Edwin, was there with his wife and two daughters.

The vicar himself stood with his head bowed while the squire shivered beside him.

Dr Philpotts, Bishop of Berham, was conducting the funeral service. His thin voice rose and fell on the icy wind.

'I know that my Redeemer liveth, and that He shall stand at the latter day upon the earth. And though after my skin worms destroy this body yet in my flesh shall I see God: whom I shall see for myself, and mine eyes shall behold, and not another.'

'There was nothing I could do, Lord,' muttered the Reverend Charles Armitage under his breath. 'There wasn't no way a man could get her to stop taking the muck without watching her day and night. All the women addle their brains with suchlike potions. How was I to *know?* I was a good husband . . . well, as good as a man could expect to be. I didn't beat her.'

'. . . every man living is altogether vanity,' intoned Dr Philpotts.

What had happened? That was the thought running through the heads of all the sisters. Could we have done anything? Did she have to die so that we would take notice of her? Only Annabelle thought rebelliously, 'How could we care for her when she never seemed to care for us?'

Two latecomers joined the mourners around the grave—Colonel Brian and Lady Godolphin.

Minerva alone remembered their mother when she had been more alive, less drugged, almost frivolous. She closed her eyes in pain and her husband, Lord Sylvester Comfrey, edged his way to her side.

'O death, where is thy sting? O grave, where is thy victory?'

'Soon we shall throw earth on the coffin,' thought Diana. 'I hope I do not faint. I cannot bear the sound.'

But soon the ceremony was performed and Dr Philpotts began to deliver the collect. The worst was over.

By the time the mourners filed two by two from the graveside, each one began to experience a sense of relief. Left behind in the grave was someone waiting peacefully in a deep sleep for the last trump.

Mrs Armitage would rest in her grave as she had rested so many times in her bedroom upstairs in the vicarage. Only Frederica, overcome with cold and misery and a dread of going back to school, let out a hysterical laugh and said to Diana that at least they would no longer have to climb the stairs to visit mother, all they had to do was walk across the churchyard. Diana hugged her and told her she should go to bed as soon as they got home. Betty, their former maid, came up and led Frederica away.

In the vicarage, the sisters sipped negus and talked in hushed voices. Minerva said that little Charles was fully recovered and she was anxious to return to him. Then she turned to Diana. 'Would you care to come to London with me, Diana?' she asked. 'There is no need for you to stay with Lady Godolphin.'

Diana shook her head. She was thinking of Mr Emberton. He must have seen her talking to Lord Dantrey that morning in the square. If she stayed in Hopeworth, then he might return. And by staying in Hopeworth, there was no danger of meeting Lord Dantrey. Then she looked across the room and gasped.

'What is *he* doing here?' she asked.

Minerva followed her gaze. Lord Dantrey stood talking to her husband, Lord Comfrey, and to Annabelle's husband, the Marquess of Brabington.

'That must be Lord Dantrey,' said Minerva, who still made it her business to know every newcomer to the neighbourhood. 'It is only natural that he should call to pay his respects. I saw him at the graveside. No doubt Sylvester invited him. You look quite white, Diana. Is anything the matter?'

Diana bit her lip and shook her head.

'And those must be the Carters,' she heard Minerva say.

Diana looked up again.

Ann Carter and her mother had entered the room. They were talking to Mr Armitage and then to Sir Edwin. Ann was wearing a silvery grey dress, so fine it could have been woven from cobwebs. Her only covering was the gauziest sort of pelisse. She looked like a fairy, dainty and fragile. Lord Dantrey was being introduced. Mrs Carter was gushing up at him, words pouring out from between her rouged lips, while all the while Lord Dantrey watched Ann. Diana saw the warmth and admiration in his eyes and felt sick.

How right she had been not to marry him. Once a rake, always a rake!

Two months later, Daphne Garfield called on her sister, Minerva. Winter still held the land in its grip; it was a bitter, dirty day with wreaths of fog sliding around the buildings.

Minerva was spending a few weeks in town to shop for her children and her household. Although she had an army of servants, she still liked to attend to domestic matters herself.

After gossip had been exchanged, Daphne got down to the purpose of her visit. 'It is Diana who concerns me,' she said. 'We were travelling back from the country and I asked Simon if we could visit Papa. It was all quite terrible. Papa has lost weight and spends a great deal of time in the church, which is where he is supposed to be, but it does not seem to bring him any consolation. I fear he blames himself sorely for Mama's death.'

'As we all do,' sighed Minerva. 'How could we be so stupid as to take her behaviour for granted? How is Diana?'

'Ah, that is the thing that is most worrying. She has become grim and gaunt and seems to do nothing but sit about the house or go for solitary walks. She shows no interest in hunting . . .'

'Nor should she,' said Minerva severely. 'Hunting is not a sport for a lady and I often think it is no sport for a gentleman.'

Daphne coloured faintly. 'Don't prose at me, Merva, for I must tell you about this. I managed to get Papa to give his permission to let Diana hunt. It was just before I married Simon. He said she could, provided she dressed as a man.'

'But she didn't!'

'She did, and it's no use glaring at me, Merva, because Diana lives for the hunt.'

'But if it should ever come out . . .'

'It has. It did. Squire Radford recognized her on the hunting field and so she was sent to Lady Godolphin to prepare for a Season. Now there seems to be no hope of a Season because of Mama's death.' Daphne clasped her hands together and gazed beseechingly at her sister. 'We must encourage Diana to hunt again, Minerva. It is the only thing that will bring both Diana and Papa out of their misery.'

'I could not countenance such a thing!'

'If Squire Radford knew, then some of the country people must have known about Diana hunting as well. So before it gets about that she hunted dressed as a man, I thought we should send her a very modish hunting dress and a side saddle. Don't you see? It would be considered very odd for Diana to hunt *at all*, but since she will be seen to be hunting in the proper style of dress, it will not be such a scandal.'

'I cannot give permission . . .'

'Stuff! I am not asking for your permission, Minerva. I am a married lady now, and if you will not help me, then I shall send Diana a riding habit myself. But if *you* were to send it, it would have great effect. Oh, I don't think poor Diana will *ever* marry. She said she hated men.'

Minerva still protested, but the beautiful and normally gentle Daphne could be very stubborn. A crash and a wail from the nursery above suddenly made Minerva say impatiently, 'Oh, very well. If Diana is as bad as you say, then I do not suppose her riding with the hunt with her father's pack in a country parish can be so very shocking. I must go to the nursery. *Yes*, Daphne, I will order a riding habit as soon as possible!'

Diana wandered aimlessly about the countryside, though any time she found her steps taking her in the direction of Saxon Mere, she swerved away and hurried off in the opposite direction. Mr Emberton, rumour had it, had returned to Wentwater mansion, but he had not attended church and was to be seen over in Hopeminster a great deal. There were rumours that Lord Dantrey was courting Miss Ann Carter. Diana felt very alone. Her father was strange and withdrawn. Normally, she would have turned to Squire Radford for help, but she blamed the little squire for Frederica's banishment to school and for the end to her own hunting days.

She was returning from one of these long walks when she felt the slightly warmer breath of the wind on her cheek, heralding an end to the frost which had held the land in an iron grip for so long. Hounds would be howling in their kennels, sensing the return of good hunting weather.

She saw a thin spiral of smoke rising from a stand of trees and her step faltered. Gypsies! She walked forward a little and stood staring. The old woman who had foretold the arrival of Jack Emberton in her life was stirring something in an iron pot slung over a fire. She looked up and beckoned to Diana to approach.

'I met the dark and handsome man you spoke of,' said Diana breathlessly. 'He came into my life but then he went away again.'

'Give me some silver and I will tell you all,' said the old witch. Her eyes were red-rimmed with smoke. Diana gave a superstitious shiver.

'Very well,' she said. She produced a shilling and held it up. The gypsy snatched it up and put it carefully away in a leather bag slung around her scrawny neck.

'Now come close, sweet life,' said the gypsy. Diana nervously sat down on an upturned cask beside the fire and held out her hand. The gypsy looked down at it and then, raising her eyes, fixed Diana with a strangely hypnotic stare.

'He ain't gone,' she said, 'your dark lover. Biding his time, that's what he's doing, on account of a death in your family.'

Diana gave a little hiss of dread and tried to pull her hand away, but the gypsy held it tight. 'He'll come back, never fear,' said the gypsy, 'if that white-haired villain don't stop him.'

'Dantrey!' gasped Diana. She wrenched her hand away and began to run as hard as she could, her hands up to her ears to drown the gypsy woman's jeering cackles of laughter.

The gypsy woman turned as her husband climbed down from the cart. 'I said my piece to the gentry mort,' she said, still laughing. 'I told her what the gentleman paid me to say.'

Diana was still shaking when she arrived home. But after a while, when her superstitious panic had subsided, she began to find comfort in what the gypsy had said. Mr Emberton had only behaved like the gentleman he was. *He* had not come to the funeral like some vulture, like Lord Dantrey. He had merely stayed away out of a delicacy of feeling. Then she caught sight of herself in the glass.

Her tanned face, surrounded with tangled elf locks, stared back at her. Her dress hung on her thin figure. What man would *want* to see her?

For the first time since the funeral Diana began to feel ravenously hungry. Unlike her other sisters, she had taught herself to cook, and cook well. All the sisters could take their turn in the kitchen if need be, but none had mastered the mysterious art of bringing a tempting meal to the table.

Diana resolved to turn the cook-house-keeper, Mrs Hammer, out of the kitchen for the rest of the day. Let her enjoy a rest. She, Diana, would set a dinner on the table tonight that would cheer her gloomy father and put some much-needed flesh on her own bones.

On impulse, she sent the odd-man over to Squire Radford with an invitation to dine. If the squire could lighten her father's grief with his usual good sense, then it was silly to continue to hold a grudge against him because of the ban on hunting.

Diana busied herself in the kitchen all afternoon. As she worked away, she muttered under her breath at her father's parsimony. Surely the vicarage finances could have run to a closed range!

Mrs Hammer had never been famous for her cooking but Diana thought, for the first time, that perhaps Mrs Hammer might improve if she did not have to work on such antiquated equipment.

The open wood fire had a hot water boiler on the right hand hob and a tiny oven on the left. The oven was not much use, and so Diana had to light a fire under the bread oven, a cast iron safe of a thing sunk into the wall.

She decided to make a hare and pigeon pie, and, after she had cleaned a large hare and two pigeons, she jointed them and put them in a pot of boiling waiter which she swung out over the fire on a crane which looked like a little black iron gallows.

Then she put a leg of mutton to roast on the spit which was down in the front of the fire, parallel to the high fender. She wound up its clockwork mechanism, thanking God for small mercies, and reflecting it was a wonder her father had not thought to use a pair of hounds to turn the spit.

While the ingredients for the pie were cooking, Diana took out a battered notebook and looked up a recipe for pudding. It seemed to involve using a great amount of raisins, currants and dates as well as flour and suet. Only when she had it all mixed and ready to put in the pot, wrapped in a cloth, to boil after the pie ingredients had cooked, did she realize she had used all the flour. There would not be any left for the pie crust. Then she remembered the genius of Mr Wedgwood and sighed with relief. At the height of the Napoleonic wars flour was very scarce indeed and Wedgwood had produced a beautifully designed crock in the shape of a pie with a raised and ornamented china crust as a lid. Minerva had presented the vicarage with one of these wonders. All Diana had to do was to fill the crock with the hare and pigeon and put on the china top and hope the gentlemen would be so pleased with the effect that they would not miss the pastry.

What with cooking and baking and pumping water from the pump over the stone sink in the scullery into buckets, the afternoon flew past and Diana realized with a sort of wondering surprise that she had started to sing as she worked.

The vicar was surprised to meet Squire Radford in the lane outside the village. He had kept clear of the squire of late feeling bitterly that his uneasy conscience did not need any further jabs.

'Evening, Jimmy,' he said awkwardly. 'Where bound?'

'Why! To dinner with you. Diana invited me.'

'*Diana!* Well, come along in. You know what Mrs Hammer's cooking is like so you'll know what to expect. I might find a good bottle of hock in the cellar to take away the taste. I think some of it's left from . . .' He had been about to say 'from the funeral' but found he could not go on.

The squire was much alarmed at the vicar's appearance. His clothes hung on his normally tubby figure and his little shoe button eyes were lustreless in his doughy face.

'Someone's singing,' said the squire as the vicar fumbled with the latch of the door. 'And I must say, Charles, there is a lovely smell coming from the kitchens.'

'Aye,' said the vicar dully. 'I've known the smell to be the only good thing about it.'

The vicar ushered the squire into the dark hall. A huge box decorated with coloured ribbons stood on the floor.

'What's this?' demanded the vicar as Sarah helped him off with his coat.

'Box from Lady Sylvester for Miss Diana.'

'Minerva, heh! Why hasn't Diana opened it?'

'Hasn't had time, master,' giggled Sarah. 'Miss Diana's been in the kitchen all afternoon, cooking dinner. Her has sent Mrs Hammer away for the day.'

'Diana can't cook,' snorted the vicar.

'Miss Diana was the one that did them cakes for the church party last year, sir,' said Sarah. 'They were very good.'

'Cakes is one thing, meat's another,' growled the vicar. 'Bring us some wine and tell Miss Diana that if she's ruined the dinner not to hide in the kitchen, but come and confess before it's too late to find something else to eat. I'm blessed if I know when I last felt hungry, Jimmy, but I would not want you to go to bed without your supper.'

The two men sat down by the fire in the vicarage parlour to fortify themselves with wine.

When a much-flushed Diana eventually summoned them to the dining table, they were prepared for the worst. The vicar thought it a bad sign that Diana was having the pudding served first, a country custom to take the sharp edge of the appetite away so that the guests would not be too hungry when it came to the main part of the meal.

Rose, Sarah and John Summer were delighted with Miss Diana's rise in spirits and all had elected to wait at table.

The vicar cautiously tasted a mouthful of pudding and his eyebrows rose in surprise. From that moment he began to eat steadily and he almost had tears in his eyes when he savoured the roast mutton delicately flavoured with dried mint. Since the vicarage still boasted old-fashioned two-pronged forks, he ate his peas by shovelling them into his mouth with his knife.

All through the meal the squire kept up a flow of amusing anecdote about what had been going on in the village, knowing full well that neither Diana nor her father had taken much interest in anything since the funeral.

'Ah, Diana,' sighed the vicar, pushing himself back a little from the table to allow room for his comfortably extended stomach, 'a girl who can cook like that belongs with the angels.'

'Most excellent,' said the squire, dabbing his mouth with his napkin, and then surreptitiously dabbing at the corners of his eyes, for he found it moving to see both father and daughter beginning to look like their normal selves.

'Hey! You shall stay with us this night and take wine, Diana,' said the vicar. 'And bring that there box from Minerva in and let's see what she has sent you.'

Diana went out into the hall and came back with John Summer and the odd-man carrying the box between them. She carefully removed the ribbon. It was so pretty that Diana thought she would send it to Frederica.

She opened the box and slowly lifted out a riding habit. It was of purple cloth frogged with gold. There was a dashing shako to go with it and a pair of riding boots. Underneath, at the very bottom, gleamed a shiny new side saddle.

'There's a letter with it,' said Diana. 'It's addressed to you, Papa.'

The vicar took the letter and broke open the seal which bore the Comfrey arms.

He read the letter several times and then handed it silently to Squire Radford.

'Dear Papa,' Minerva had written. 'I was much Distressed when Daphne told me that Diana had been *hunting dressed as a man.*

Daphne also told me that Diana is Much Altered in Appearance through Grief. I think you will find it is known in the county that Diana *Hunts*. It must be forgotten as *quickly as possible* that she has been seen in men's clothes. Although I know hunting is not a Ladylike Sport, it is better to have a modicum of scandal to oust a larger one. To this end, I am sending Diana this riding dress, together with a side saddle. I think it would benefit her spirits greatly to go out with the Hunt. It is not as if she can enjoy a Season this year with Mama so lately put to rest . . .'

The rest of the letter dealt mainly with gossip about the vicar's grandsons.

'Why not?' said the squire. 'I think Minerva has shown very good sense. There will be a few raised eyebrows. But provided Diana learns to behave in a feminine and graceful way in company, I see no harm in allowing her to join the hunt. I know you have not taken hounds out, Charles, due to respect for your wife. But poor Mrs Armitage would be distressed if she could see you both in such a miserable state.'

The squire had had a quick wrestle with his conscience before he said this. But he had decided it was surely better to have Diana the Huntress back, glowing and healthy, than the grim, gaunt Diana who had haunted the vicarage and the surrounding countryside for the past two months.

'What is all this about, Papa?' asked Diana.

'Show her the letter, Jimmy,' said the vicar.

Diana read the beginning of the letter over and over again. Then she fingered the fine material of the modish riding habit, a flush of excitement creeping up her thin cheeks. 'The frost has gone, Papa,' she said slowly. 'It will be good hunting weather tomorrow.'

'I promised . . .' began the vicar and then looked like a sulky child.

'Giving up your hunting, Charles, will not bring Mrs Armitage back,' said the squire gently. 'Your low spirits have affected your household and your parishioners. It is now time to go on living.'

The vicar rang the bell. 'Send John Summer back in,' he said to Sarah. When John entered the room, the vicar said, 'We ride out tomorrow, John. We'll get that old fox yet.'

'Right, sir,' said John, beaming all over his

face. 'I'll put the word about. Farmer Blake will want to come and that Mr Emberton over at the Wentwater place as well.'

'Forget Mr Emberton for the moment, John,' said the vicar.

Diana's face lost some of its brightness.

But the vicar did not want any eligible man to see his daughter on the hunting field.

CHAPTER SEVEN

Lord Dantrey was driving along a country lane the following afternoon with Miss Ann Carter by his side. He wished she would not talk. When she did, he found himself becoming restless and bored. When she did not open her mouth, he was enchanted again by her fairy-like appearance. Also, when she was silent, he was able to indulge himself by comparing her favourably with the hoydenish and eccentric Miss Armitage. He did not consider the Carters very good *ton*. On the other hand, he had decided to settle down and get married. He had reached that dangerous state of mind where a gentleman is likely to propose marriage to a highly unsuitable female. The same disease often afflicts quite sensible ladies. The Titanias of this world do not need magic to make them fall in love with the nearest ass. The survival instinct demands that we rush to get married, often at the wrong time and to the wrong person.

Apart from any other reason, he quite simply wanted Miss Ann Carter in his bed. He had been very correct in his behaviour and had not even pressed her hand. What Miss Ann lacked in conversation she made up for in the art of dress. Although the day was very cold, she seemed content to wear the lightest of wraps, and had a way of leaning forward to tighten the ribbons of her shoe with an impatient little shake which allowed Lord Dantrey the delightful sight of two firm breasts, trembling against the silk of her bodice.

'There is an assembly in Hopeminster on Saturday, my lord,' said Ann, peeping up at him from the shadow of her bonnet. 'I believe we are to be honoured with your presence.'

'I do not know if my presence will add anything much to a country ball. But since a beauty such as yourself considers it a suitable affair to attend, who am I to hold back?'

Ann laughed and preened. But her laugh was silvery and her preening involved a great deal of tossing of her golden curls against the pink of her cheeks. Lord Dantrey chided himself for being overcritical. Ann would make him a charming wife. He could court her in the country thereby saving himself the rigours of a Season in town.

Then they heard the belling of hounds and the high winding note of a huntsman's horn.

'Coming this way,' said Lord Dantrey, reining in his team.

His sharp ears told him that hounds were in full cry. With any luck, they would come crashing through the hedge onto the road and Ann would squeak with fright and throw herself into his arms. As a matter of fact, Ann was sitting demurely beside him, waiting for an opportunity to do just that.

Hounds came thrusting through a gap in the hedge and streamed across the road, disappearing through a break in the wall on the other side.

'When the first huntsman comes over the hedge, I will pretend to be frightened,' thought Ann.

Magnificent in her new purple riding habit, Diana Armitage cleared the hedge. Ann let out a shrill cry and threw herself into Lord Dantrey's arms. His hands did not leave the reins. He sat very still.

Annoyed, Ann sat up, her cheeks very flushed.

She had not seen Diana, but Lord Dantrey most certainly had. The riding habit fitted Diana like a glove and the dashing shako balanced neatly on her glossy curls. The other huntsmen, led by the vicar, were emerging through a gap in the hedge further up the road; obviously no one else had dared to make the same dramatic jump as Diana.

'Miss Diana seems to be recovering from the shock of her mother's death,' said Lord Dantrey.

'I have not seen her,' said Ann crossly, straightening her bonnet. 'I wished to call but Mama said . . .' She bit her lip. Mama had actually said there was no use working up a friendship with the gauche Diana when that young lady was immersed in gloom in a country vicarage and would not be in London for the Season.

'Diana the Huntress,' smiled Lord Dantrey. 'I must say, she looked magnificent.'

'When?' demanded Ann, an edge to her voice.

'Just now. She was leading the hunt.'

'How *terrible*,' breathed Ann. 'A woman *hunting*. She must be as coarse as Letty Lade.'

'On the contrary, she may well set the fashion if she continues to look so modish,' said Lord Dantrey.

Ann bristled like a little kitten. 'Do not tell me you *approve* of ladies hunting, my lord!'

'Not in the slightest. I do not know of any other lady of my acquaintance who could carry it off with the same air as Miss Diana.'

Ann pouted. She prided herself on her horsemanship. But she did not want to hunt. Perhaps she might have to, if only for a little. Lord Dantrey's taste in females might prove to run to Amazons.

'Faith, this is a gloomy place,' complained Mr Emberton as he sat with his friend, Peter Flanders, in the cold library of the Wentwater mansion.

'Then why do we stay?' demanded Mr Flanders petulantly. 'It's not as if you show any interest in Miss Armitage. Your recent game of fleecing young Barnaby Jones has been profitable. But he's cleaned out, and his father's taken him off to London.'

'I beat him fairly and squarely at hazard. I did not fleece him, as you so nastily put it.'

'You'd never have thought of him if I hadn't found out he was a rich merchant's son with more money than sense,' said Mr Flanders proudly.

'Well, well. So be it. I have not given up Miss Armitage. I kept clear. First, because I feared she would wed Dantrey after all. I mean, what the deuce was she doing talking to him in the middle of Hanover Square at that hour of the morning? Secondly, because of her mother's death. Girls in mourning don't come a-courting. But I have not forgotten her. She seems to be superstitious and believes in all that rubbish the Egyptians talk. That's why I stopped to talk to that old beldame. I told her if she saw Miss Diana to read her palm and say I had not forgot her. The gypsy told Diana Armitage that a dark and handsome lover was to come into her life, and Miss Diana thinks that's me,' said Mr Emberton smugly.

'There's a ball on Saturday.'

'A country hop. Pooh!'

'A lot of the county notables are to be there. And there might be easier, fairer game for you.'

'Who?'

'A Miss Ann Carter.' Mr Flanders kissed his fingers. 'A diamond of the first water. Rich widowed mother guards the treasure.

Bit of a dragon.'

'Aha! Perhaps I might go to this dance after all. I do not suppose Miss Diana will go. She is still in mourning.'

'Oh, she can go all right so long as she does not dance.'

Mr Emberton bit his thumb nail and sat for a few moments, buried in thought. 'Will Dantrey be there?'

'Don't suppose he'd lower himself. Very high in the instep is Dantrey.'

'I think perhaps I might pay a call on the vicarage,' said Mr Emberton thoughtfully. 'Someone over in Hopeminster said Miss Diana was looking plain and ill. She might be even readier to fall into my arms.'

'What if she told her father about the elopement?'

'Then he would have been around here waving his horsewhip. Miss Diana has kept quiet about it. Furthermore, Dantrey don't want to marry her. Stands to reason he must have withstood all sorts of pressures so everyone's keeping quiet about everything.'

'Don't take me with you,' said Mr Flanders. 'Can't stand vicars.'

Mr Emberton rode over to the vicarage in the dim light of late afternoon. Sarah answered the door since Rose was down in the village, buying ribbons.

She told Mr Emberton that everyone was out with the hunt and cast a languishing eye over his tall form.

'But if you was to step into the parlour, sir,' she said, 'you could wait till they return. Shouldn't be long now, I reckon.'

Mr Emberton looked appreciatively at Sarah's rounded figure and promptly accepted the invitation. Soon he was settled in the vicarage parlour with a glass of the vicar's best hock in his hand and his feet up on the fender. He was just wondering whether to ring the bell to summon Sarah and see if he could steal a kiss when he heard the hunt returning home.

He heard Sarah say something in the hall and the vicar's voice, suddenly loud, 'Damn and blast you, girl. I'm too tired to see anyone,' and then the door opened and the vicar, followed by Diana, walked into the parlour.

'You will excuse us,' said the vicar, glaring at the glass of hock in Mr Emberton's hand. 'We've had a hard ride and we must get cleaned. So if you don't mind . . .'

'I shall call another time,' said Mr

Emberton hastily. He looked at Diana who lowered her eyes and bit her lip in mortification. A pheasant had rocketed up, right at Blarney's feet, causing the mare to rear and throw her. Diana had landed slap in a bog, face down. Her beautiful new habit was smeared with black mud and her hat was crushed. There was a streak of mud on her face. 'I was wondering whether we could look forward to the pleasure of seeing Miss Diana at the ball on Saturday,' said Mr Emberton.

'We're in mourning, or had you forgotten,' snapped the vicar.

'I thought Miss Diana could come for a little and watch the dancers,' said Mr Emberton.

'Well, think again,' growled the vicar rudely.

'It is very kind of you to call, Mr Emberton,' said Diana hurriedly. 'As you can see, we are not in a state to receive visitors.' She threw a defiant look at her father. 'Perhaps I may go to the ball after all.'

She moved towards Mr Emberton, her large eyes fixed on his face. She walked straight into the arm of an old-fashioned sofa and tumbled headlong onto it.

'Clumsy sheep, that's what you are,' said the vicar nastily. He was in a bad mood for the village boys had dragged red herrings across the scent and so hounds had lost the fox.

'I think I had better go,' said Mr Emberton. 'I hope to see you on Saturday.'

'Oh, go on with you,' said the vicar crossly. Mr Emberton helped Diana to her feet and smiled at her, affecting not to hear.

In the hall, he took his hat and his cane from a smiling Sarah, and, quickly looking around, he bent and kissed her on the cheek.

'Lawks, sir!' said Sarah with a giggle. 'Master's as cross as crabs. Better not let him catch you.'

'Not me,' grinned Mr Emberton, feeling his spirits restored. 'See if you can get your mistress to go to the ball.'

'And what do I get if I do?' asked Sarah.

'Another kiss.'

'Pooh, kisses is ten a penny.'

'Then I shall kiss you twelve times and that makes a shilling.'

Mr Emberton mounted his horse outside and cantered off, happily aware that the pretty maid was standing in the open doorway, watching him.

'It would be much more conventional for me to appear at a ball, Papa,' Diana Armitage was saying furiously as Mr Emberton rode away, 'than to go hunting.'

But the vicar thought his bad day's hunting had been a punishment from the Almighty for trying to enjoy himself so soon after his wife's death. In his way he was as superstitious as Diana, and his God was more Greek than Christian, sending down thunderbolts of misery as punishment, and dispensing very little love and charity to the sinner.

Sarah appeared, looking flushed and still giggling. Diana threw her a suspicious look, but the vicar brightened perceptibly.

'Mr Emberton do be hoping hard that Miss Diana will be at the ball Saturday,' said Sarah.

'Well, she ain't going, and what were you about to give that fellow my best hock?' said the vicar.

'First thing came to hand, and Rose is down in the village,' said Sarah pertly. 'You said I was to be lady's maid,' she added in a wheedling tone, 'but I don't have much practice, and it would be fine to prettify miss for the ball. Not as if Miss Diana had to dance. And that semi-mourning gown Miss Annabelle sent is so very beautiful.'

She fluttered her eyelashes at the vicar who looked sheepishly at his daughter.

'I suppose it couldn't do no harm,' said the vicar. 'Squire and myself might take you along, Diana, and that'll make it right and tight.'

The vicarage was very silent as Diana sat in front of the dressing table, preparing for the ball. She could not help but remember brighter, happier days when the house was full of noise and excitement with all the sisters gossiping and chattering as they prepared themselves for an evening in Hopeminster.

The closed door of her late mother's room was foremost in her mind. It had been closed so often in former days, Mrs Armitage lying behind it in bed in a drugged sleep. It was hard to pass that room and know that its one-time occupant was lying in the churchyard. She wondered what her mother had really thought about; what her worries and fears had been and whether any of them could have done anything to stop her treating herself with those awful medicines.

A full moon riding high in the sky sent sparks of light twinkling over the frost-covered garden. There was no wind and the tall candles on the dressing table burned bright and clear.

Diana's gown was of grey silk trimmed with black ribbons. Dull red silk roses and black ribbons were threaded through in her hair. She felt she looked like a dowager, but Sarah was pleased with the effect. Her eyes were enormous in her thin face and Sarah thought the sombre colours made Diana look much more dramatic than any fashionable debutante pastel would have done.

Sarah put a cape of crushed velvet about Diana's shoulders and declared her ready to go downstairs to join the squire and her father.

It was a relief to leave the vicarage with all its sadness and silence and go bowling along the frosty, sparkling road from Hopeworth to the county town of Hopeminster under a full moon and a starry sky.

The squire was resplendent in antique finery, the lace at his wrists and throat as fine as cobwebs. The vicar was in good spirits, for he had discovered his evening dress fitted his now thinner figure and so he had not had to put on corsets. The squire wore his hair powdered and his wrinkled face was delicately painted. Old habits die hard and the squire never considered himself dressed for a ball without powder and paint.

Diana began to feel tremors of excitement. She would see Mr Emberton again, see his laughing blue eyes and feel his reassuring presence. Certainly it was strange that he had not managed to send her a letter explaining why he had departed so quickly on the day of their planned elopement. Even though one knew the reason was bound to have been the presence of Lord Dantrey, it would have been a gentlemanly thing to have at least tried to send some sort of explanation, some love letter.

But he had stayed away, surely, because of her mother's death, Diana reminded herself severely. Lord Dantrey had come to the funeral but he had made no attempt to speak to her.

Her excitement grew as the silhouettes of the towers and spires of Hopeminster rose above the flat fields.

The assembly was being held in the Cock and Feathers. As they drove into the courtyard Diana could hear the music of the fiddles and the beat-beat-beat of the drum. She was relieved that her mourning state stopped her from dancing. Diana had had dancing lessons in London when she was staying with her sisters, but the dancing master, a very excitable Frenchman, had been barely five feet high. He had made her feel so nervous that she had hardly been able to learn any of the steps, and then she was never quite sure which was her left foot and which her right. The dancing master had tied different coloured ribbons on each slipper to help her, but every time she looked down at her feet to tell the left from the right by the colour of the ribbons, she fell over him.

It was when she had returned to Minerva's from one of these lessons, demanding, 'Pray, what is the meaning of "merde"?' that dancing instruction had mysteriously ended.

She left her cape in an ante room and adjusted a few curls in the mirror, surprised and pleased with her appearance. She could hardly believe the elegant beauty staring back at her was her own reflection.

And then the first person she saw on entering the ballroom was Ann Carter. She was dancing with Mr Emberton, his large size making Ann seem even more diminutive and fragile. She was dressed in a filmy thing of pink and silver gauze. Her hair gleamed in the candlelight like newly-minted guineas. Her little feet barely seemed to touch the floor.

Feeling once more like a great lumbering giant, Diana found herself placed on a row of chairs against the wall. Squire Radford sat and talked to her for a few moments and then left to fetch her a glass of lemonade.

Diana played with the sticks of her fan. The music sounded so jolly and everyone seemed to be dancing with such ease. All at once she longed to dance herself, to float like Ann Carter through the mazy steps of the quadrille.

She raised her head at the final chord of the music. Surely he would approach her now. She remembered the gypsy's words and felt comforted.

Mr Emberton was promenading with Ann on his arm. She looked across the room, saw Diana sitting against the wall and said something to Mr Emberton. He glanced at Diana and he *laughed*. Diana flushed. She wondered miserably whether her appearance at a ball so soon after her mother's death was considered odd; whether that was what had caused Ann to comment and Mr Emberton to laugh.

Squire Radford returned with her lemonade. 'If you will excuse me, Miss Diana,' he said, handing her the glass. 'There is an old friend here I have not seen this age. I do not wish to leave you alone . . .'

'I am enjoying watching the dancers,' said Diana. 'I will do very well.'

The squire bowed and left. Diana looked down into her glass of lemonade. The music struck up again and she covertly looked up again. *Now* he would come. Please God. If the log in the fireplace which looked just about ready to fall down into the hot ash and flare up stayed where it was, *then* he would come. She would concentrate on watching the log. The log fell. A cheerful blaze roared up the chimney.

'Miss Armitage.'

Stars in her eyes and a blush of pleasure on her cheeks, Diana looked up.

Lord Dantrey stood looking down at her.

Her face fell.

He pulled forward a chair and sat next to

her. 'I was extremely sorry to hear of your mother's death,' he said, his voice as pleasant and husky as ever. 'You may have seen me at the funeral. I did not approach you for fear I would upset you further. It is a hard time for you.'

'Thank you, my lord,' said Diana primly.

'May I hope that you will honour me with one dance?'

'I am afraid I must refuse,' said Diana. 'I am in mourning.'

'As everyone knows. I took the liberty of asking the Master of Ceremonies if it would be very shocking if I were to lead you to the floor and he said "not at all". Your family is much respected in the neighbourhood and everyone, it seems, would be happy to see you enjoying yourself.'

Diana mumbled something and he inclined his head. 'I beg your pardon, Miss Armitage.'

Diana felt hot and awkward. She could not bear to look at him. If only he would go *away*. 'I am perfectly all right, sir,' she said, her voice sounding unnaturally loud in her own ears.

She raised her head and looked across the ballroom—and straight into the angry eyes of Ann Carter. Mr Emberton was handing her something to drink and he, too, was looking to where Diana sat with Lord Dantrey. Several other young ladies were staring at Diana with jealous, speculative eyes.

Diana looked properly at her companion for the first time that evening.

His white-gold hair was impeccably dressed and the black cloth of his evening coat was stretched across his shoulders without a wrinkle. His silver and white striped waistcoat sported diamond studs and a large diamond pin winked in the snowy folds of his intricately tied cravat. He made every other man in the room look provincial and dowdy.

Diana felt an angry little glow inside. If the company of Lord Dantrey caused such speculation and envy in the eyes of the company, then she could make full use of it.

She smiled blindingly up at Lord Dantrey. 'I must apologize for my awkward be-haviour,' she said. 'I am a little afraid of you—afraid that you might speak about my escapade.'

'You make it very hard to remember,' smiled Lord Dantrey, well aware of the reason for Miss Armitage's sudden good nature. 'I entertained a callow youth called David Armitage in London. He bears no resemblance to the radiant beauty beside me tonight.'

Diana tried to give an imitation of Ann's silvery laugh. Then she rapped Lord Dantrey playfully on the knuckles with the sticks of her fan. Unfortunately, she did not know her own strength and the ivory sticks made a thwacking sound as they came down on the back of his hand. He rubbed his hand and wondered why he had felt compelled to talk to her. The pretty Ann was casting languishing looks in his direction. If he paid Diana another compliment, he felt sure she was quite capable of slapping him on the back with enough force to send him flying across the ballroom. But her lips had been delicious. He frowned at that thought. Diana Armitage would not make a suitable wife. Ann Carter would. He was wasting his time.

But he knew that the waltz was to be danced after the present country dance was over, and the urge to take her in his arms again defied all logic.

He talked lightly and easily of his plans to improve the old Osbadiston estates and, as he talked about his concern for his tenants, Diana realized with a pang of conscience that she had not visited any of the parishioners. Even Daphne at her most vain had still gone about the duties of the parish.

After the funeral Minerva had gone to see them all, asking particularly after Mrs Jones's sickly baby. Then she, Diana, had not written to poor little Frederica since the funeral. She would sit down that very night before she went to bed and tell Frederica all about the ball.

'I asked you if you thought it would be a good idea, Miss Diana, and you scowled. Does that mean you consider my plan frivolous?'

'I am sorry,' said Diana, blushing, 'I was not listening.'

Lord Dantrey looked at her with some amusement. 'You are most refreshing, Miss Diana, and very good for me. I had become quite puffed up in mine own conceit. It is a wonderful thing to be rich and titled. The ladies of the county hang on my every word.'

'You were talking about the welfare of your tenants,' said Diana, feeling too embarrassed to do other than tell the truth, 'and I began to think of all the parish duties

I had neglected. Poor Mr Pettifor. That's our curate. He works very hard and I am afraid we take him for granted. Minerva, my eldest sister, did such a lot of work before her marriage. She organized the Poor Fund and she never failed to visit the sick.'

'Perhaps it might enable you to overcome some of the grief of your bereavement if you had more to do,' said Lord Dantrey, looking at her curiously.

'Perhaps. You must forgive me, my lord. I had not meant to be so serious.'

'One should always be serious about things that matter. I was talking of lighter things when you were not listening. I was wondering whether to hold a ball myself. Can I not persuade you to accompany me in the waltz, Miss Diana? It is the next dance.'

Diana opened her mouth to refuse but, at that moment, she saw Mr Emberton bend his black curls over Ann's fair ones and say something which made that young lady laugh.

'Thank you, my lord,' said Diana. 'Yes, I have decided to dance.'

'It is only a dance,' he teased. 'Not a walk to the scaffold. You look quite grim. Tell me about Mr Emberton.'

'What is there to say?'

'Volumes. Did he flee the square because of my presence?'

'I do not know. I would rather forget about the whole thing.'

'But he no doubt called to explain his behaviour.'

'How could he? He is a gentleman of delicacy and refinement. He is staying away because of my recent bereavement. The gypsy said . . .'

'Gypsy! What gypsy?'

'Nothing,' mumbled Diana.

'Aha! You have been talking to the gypsies in the wood and they told you you were to meet a dark and handsome man. They always say that,' he mocked. 'What lady was ever told she was about to meet a tall, fair man?'

'I believe her!" said Diana, goaded into indiscretion. 'And she knew of you because she warned me that a white-haired villain might try to stop me.'

'Tell me more. You must, you know. Come! Convert the unbeliever.'

His green and gold eyes under their heavy lids were mocking, teasing.

Diana gritted her teeth. 'Very well. I

shall.' She told him about the first meeting with the gypsy, and then the second.

'The first,' said Lord Dantrey coldly, 'was simply something that gypsies always say to gullible females. The second? You interest me. I think you will find that Mr Emberton crossed the gypsy's palm with silver before you even got there. I am amazed that a sensible female such yourself should believe such rubbish.'

'How would Mr Emberton know anything about the gypsies at Hopeworth?'

'Because, I should think, you told him.'

'I did not!' said Diana, and then blushed painfully, for all at once she remembered telling Mr Emberton about the gypsy that evening at Lady Godolphin's.

Lord Dantrey raised his quizzing glass and studied Mr Emberton. A small court of gentlemen had formed about Ann but Mr Emberton was managing to engage most of her attention. He felt, all at once, a deep concern for Diana's welfare. He did not like this Emberton, nor did he trust him. Had he shown by one flicker of an eyelid that he was deeply in love with Diana, then Lord Dantrey would have been content to let the comedy run its course. But Emberton was an adventurer. The Armitages were not famous for their wealth. Perhaps Mr Emberton was playing that old game of hoping to be bought off by the wealthy relatives. Lord Dantrey was not worried about Ann Carter's affections straying from himself. Her ambitious Mama would see to that.

Therefore, it would be a good deed to put a spoke in Mr Emberton's wheel. He was sharing the Wentwater mansion with Mr Peter Flanders, a weak young man, the kind of weak young man who always attached himself to a bully or a villain or both.

'Are you *very* superstitious, Miss Diana?' he asked.

'No, my lord,' said Diana crossly. 'I simply believe there is a great deal of wisdom in old country sayings.'

'We will talk about it later,' said Lord Dantrey. 'Our dance, Miss Diana.'

He felt a stab of irritation as he sensed, rather than saw, her eyes seeking those of Mr Emberton.

'Very well, my lord.' Diana stood up and he took her arm and led her onto the floor.

By the time they had circled one half of the room, Lord Dantrey thought his feet would never be the same again. He could only be thankful that the fashion for thin silk slippers was still in vogue and that the ladies had not reverted to the high red heels of earlier times. Miss Diana Armitage seemed unable to put one foot on the ballroom floor. She seemed to prefer to dance on the top of his feet.

Then he saw Diana glance at Ann who was sailing past in the arms of a red-coated officer. Ann looked at Diana's clumsy steps and giggled. Diana blushed. She felt she had never blushed so much in her life as she was doing that evening. A tide of scalding red was rising from the soles of her feet to the top of her head.

Lord Dantrey pressed his hand firmly against the small of her back. 'Look at me, Miss Diana,' he commanded. 'Do not think of your steps. Think only that you are a beautiful and graceful woman.'

Diana looked up. His green gaze was unwavering, intent, hypnotic. She remembered the feel of his lips against her own. Her gaze fell to his mouth. 'No, look up!' he said.

Diana felt strange. The more she gazed into his eyes, the more light-headed she felt.

Faces around her swirled away in a coloured mist.

'By George,' said the officer who was dancing with Ann. 'It looks as if Dantrey has fallen at last. He can't take his eyes off that fascinating-looking girl. She dances beautifully. Who is she?'

'Diana Armitage,' said Ann crossly, stumbling over the officer's feet. 'An odd girl. She hunts.'

'Does she, by Jove!'

To Ann's intense irritation the fact that Diana hunted seemed to increase her attraction in the officer's eyes. This was what came of spending too much time with Mr Emberton. 'Mama will never forgive me an I let Lord Dantrey get away,' thought Ann. 'If only this stupid waltz would end!'

But the Master of Ceremonies had told the band to play longer than usual. He felt it was a great social coup to not only have such a personage as Lord Dantrey present at this country assembly but to have him demonstrate to everybody present just how much he was enjoying himself.

'You dance like an angel,' said Lord Dantrey to Diana, and Diana smiled dreamily up at him, held enchanted in a world of music and colour by the admiration in his eyes and the strong pressure of his hand on her waist.

When the final chord of the music sounded, she stood blinking up at him in the light. He took her arm to walk with her and found to his extreme irritation that Mr Jack Emberton was standing at his elbow.

'Forgive me for not joining you sooner,' said Mr Emberton with a proprietary air, 'I was persuaded you would not dance because of your mourning state.'

'I did not intend to,' said Diana, 'but Lord Dantrey was told by the Master of Ceremonies that it would not cause comment or offence if I did.'

'In that case, let me beg the next dance.' He laid a hand on her arm, the one that was not being held by Lord Dantrey.

'It is time for supper, Emberton,' said Lord Dantrey, 'and since I have just finished dancing with Miss Diana, mine is the honour to take her in.'

'I think Miss Carter is looking for you, my lord,' said Mr Emberton. 'I am sure she told me you had promised to take her into supper.'

'You are mistaken,' said Lord Dantrey.

'You also have your hand on Miss Diana's arm. Pray remove it immediately.'

Mr Emberton removed his hand, clenched his fists, and glared at Lord Dantrey who looked coldly back.

'Emberton,' said Lord Dantrey silkily, 'do not force me to call you out.'

Jack Emberton turned on his heel and strode away. Mrs Carter was looking daggers at him, obviously blaming him for monopolizing her daughter.

Ann was already being led into the supper room by her officer.

Emily Chesterton, Ann Carter's recently acquired 'best friend' had heard the exchange between Mr Emberton and Lord Dantrey and was busy spreading a highly-coloured account of how Lord Dantrey had challenged Mr Emberton to a duel. The news spread around the long tables of the supper room like wildfire. The county was proud of the social success of the Armitage girls and the guests were delighted that Diana appeared to be living up to the high standards of fatal female attraction already set by her elder sisters.

Lord Dantrey was amazed at the feelings that had been roused in him when Jack

Emberton had laid his hand on Diana's arm.

He did not like the way her large eyes kept straying in Mr Emberton's direction.

'You are not eating, Miss Diana,' he said.

Mr Emberton smiled down the room at Diana who smiled back.

'Your food, Miss Diana,' said Lord Dantrey acidly. 'I am persuaded a great strapping girl such as yourself must have a good appetite.' Now why had he said that? He had meant to pay her a pretty compliment.

'Excuse me, my lord,' said Diana, 'my thoughts were elsewhere.'

He would rather she had lashed out at him instead of meekly sitting there, obviously hoping the ordeal of dining with him would soon be over.

As for Diana, she found that the close proximity of Lord Dantrey was doing odd things to her body. She felt hot, then cold, and her hands had taken on a life of their own and trembled when she picked up her knife and fork. There was such a lot of food on her plate, she thought, staring down at a modest portion of meat and vegetables. It was considered good manners to put a little of everything on your plate on your fork, all at the same time—as Captain Gronow was to say later in his *Recollections,* one did all one's compound cookery between between one's jaws—so Diana took a small piece of ham, a minuscule piece of chicken, a morsel of sausage, a tiny piece of cauliflower, a sliver of the inevitable boiled potato, raised it to her mouth and then put her fork back on her plate again, the food untasted.

'You are not hungry, Miss Diana?' asked Lord Dantrey.

'I do wish you would not study me so closely,' snapped Diana. 'You are making me feel uncomfortable.'

'Then I should bribe a gypsy to tell you that I am suitable company for you,' said Lord Dantrey. 'A glass of wine?'

'No . . . I mean, yes.' Wine might give her courage. She seized the glass clumsily and it tipped over, and the contents ran along the tablecloth, spreading out into a large red stain.

Diana grabbed her napkin and began to dab at it ineffectually. He signalled to a waiter to replace her glass and then took hold of her wrist.

The touch of his hand on her skin was like a shock from one of the new electric machines that people were so fond of playing with at parties.

She yelped as if he had burned her, jerked her hand away, and sent her plate of food cascading into his lap.

'I-I am s-sorry,' babbled Diana. Eyes were on her. She could feel them. Hundreds of mocking, curious eyes. Ann Carter's silvery laugh sounded in her ears.

'Pray do not be so upset.' Lord Dantrey carefully removed all the food from his clothes, put it all neatly back on the plate, and handed the lot to the waiters who were bustling forward with fresh plates, napkins and glasses. Lord Dantrey requested a glass of soda water and, when it came, he sponged his waistcoat, working away neatly and deftly until every stain was removed.

Diana was red in the face and distressed little wisps of hair were beginning to descend about her face. Lord Dantrey sighed.

'Miss Diana,' he said in a low voice. 'I am not an ogre. I may have used you roughly once, I may have treated you to an excess of civility, but I have no intention of doing so again. You are a beautiful and desirable woman. You ride like Diana the Huntress. You have nothing to fear from me.

Do you understand?'

His eyes were upon her and she met his gaze with a troubled look. She saw only kindness and concern in his face and began to feel her hands stop trembling and her body relax.

She realized everyone in the room was talking and eating and laughing and no one was looking in their direction.

'Forgive me, Lord Dantrey,' she said, taking a sip of wine. 'I have always been clumsy. Ah, you should see my sisters, particularly Daphne. *She* never spills anything or drops anything. I am taller than my sisters and I have always felt an overgrown giant beside them.'

'One day,' said Lord Dantrey, 'you will look in the glass and see yourself for the goddess you are. Then only a duke will be good enough for you.'

'If you continue to compliment me in such a *warm* way,' laughed Diana, 'I will be persuaded that you are the rake you are said to be.'

'That would never do. My rakish days are over. I am determined to settle down and get married.'

'To Miss Carter?'

'I have not made up my mind.'

'Is it not a question of the lady making up her mind as well? Have you only to drop the handkerchief?'

'Yes.'

'Not in my case,' said Diana boldly.

'Nobody asked you.'

'I did not mean *you*, my lord. I meant that I am not like to go rushing into any man's arms simply because he does me the honour of proposing marriage.'

'But you have obviously dreamed of the ideal husband. Who is he?—this dream figure.'

Diana had been drinking steadily. A warm glow from the wine plus a lack of fear of this formidable lord was making her feel elated. 'He is tall,' she said dreamily, 'and he has black hair. He treats me as an equal. We do everything together. We hunt, we fish, we ride, we . . .'

'Make love?'

'My lord!'

'Forgive me. I could not help wondering whether the little matter of love ever entered your head.'

'I do not think love so important as . . . as equality and . . . companionship.'

'When you are telling lies, as you are doing now,' he said, 'your eyes cloud over and your lips become compressed.'

'You do not understand. I do not expect you to understand. You are very much older than I, and people of your generation have such very old-fashioned ideas.'

'I am *not* old, Miss Diana,' said Lord Dantrey, irritated. 'I am in the prime of life.'

'Your hair is white.'

'My hair is very fair as you well know, Miss Diana. Now what did I say to make you so unpleasant?'

'You annoy me, my lord,' said Diana candidly. She took a large mouthful of wine and smiled at him mistily. 'I think that to be married to you would be to give up all freedom, all independence. I would barely see you. You would spend your time at prize fights, at clubs, and the cockpit, and I would be expected to sit at home and gossip and sew, and say, "Yes, Dantrey, no, Dantrey," to all your requests. You would expect me to have a baby each year. By the time I reached your age, my lord, I should be old and worn out.'

His lips twitched. 'The idea of wearing you out is rather exciting.'

'Be serious. Think! You do not see yourself, after marriage, spending any amount of time in your wife's company.'

'Ah, but the Armitage girls are already legends. Your sisters' husbands barely stray from home.'

'My sisters are so very beautiful,' said Diana wistfully.

'You are fishing for compliments. I have already said that I find you beautiful.'

'Lord Dantrey, compliments roll so easily from your tongue that I can only come to the conclusion you have had a great deal of practice.'

'Oh, yes.'

Diana's face fell ludicrously.

'On the other hand, I meant what I said to *you.*' He put his hand on his heart and leaned towards her. 'I would that you would gaze at me as fixedly as you are gazing at your plate.'

She raised her eyes to his. She felt dizzy with the amount of wine she had drunk. In fact, she must have had too much to drink since his intent green and gold gaze was the only fixed point in a spinning room.

'Diana,' he said with a slight break in his voice. 'You . . .'

'Lord Dantrey!' Mrs Carter stood behind them. 'I am delighted to see you grace our little country affair.'

He rose to his feet. 'May I present Miss Diana Armitage. Mrs Carter, Miss Armitage, Miss Armitage, Mrs Ca . . .'

'We have met,' said Mrs Carter, flashing a wintry smile at Diana. 'I am surprised to notice that your recent sad loss does not prevent you from dancing, Miss Armitage. You are young and have no one to guide you, so I suppose it is understandable that you do not realize one must observe the conventions in the country as much as in town.'

'I obtained permission to ask Miss Armitage to dance,' said Lord Dantrey, 'from the Master of Ceremonies. Many of the local people wish Miss Armitage well and are happy to see her enjoying herself.'

Mrs Carter bit her lip in vexation. She had found that the ladies of the county's initial jealousy of Diana's seeming capture of Lord Dantrey had been quickly replaced by admiration. The local belles merely shrugged and said good-naturedly that no one had ever been a match for the Armitage girls.

She contented herself with a little bow by

way of response and then turned back to Lord Dantrey, all flashing eyes and teeth. 'My little Ann enjoyed her drive with you t'other day prodigiously.'

'The pleasure was all mine, I assure you, Mrs Carter.'

'I must send you a card. I have quite a little salon. We have cards and music.'

'Unfortunately, my duties keep me at home, Mrs Carter.'

'Ah, we will see if Ann cannot persuade you otherwise.' Mrs Carter made an urgent beckoning motion with her hand behind her back and Ann came up on the arm of her officer.

Ann edged in against the table so that she was standing with her back to Diana and facing Lord Dantrey. Lord Dantrey should have noticed this piece of rudeness, should have commented on it, thought Diana, but he was smiling down at Ann with a caressing look in his eyes. People were going back into the ballroom and the supper room was nearly empty. Diana saw Mr Emberton standing at the end of the room, watching her.

She slid out of her seat and went up to him, not aware that Lord Dantrey had stiffened, not aware that gentleman was watching her every move over the top of Ann's golden head.

Mr Emberton decided the best policy was to avoid all mention of Lord Dantrey's name. He now realized he had little hope of attracting Ann Carter, not with Lord Dantrey and her ambitious mother around. He knew Ann was already regretting spending so much time with him. So back to plan one—Diana Armitage.

'You are in looks tonight, Miss Diana,' he said with that cheerful manner of his which never failed to put her at ease. 'Now that I have you to myself, may I beg the next dance?'

Diana smiled at him brilliantly. What a contrast he was to Lord Dantrey! And who cared about Lord Dantrey anyway? Let him flirt and flatter silly misses like Ann Carter. She was welcome to him.

But somehow Diana found she could not dance with Mr Emberton. That magic which had guided her steps through the waltz had mysteriously disappeared and her old clumsiness had returned.

'I am a dreadful dancer, Mr Emberton,' she said ruefully. 'Pray let us sit down for a little. I would like something to drink. I am so very thirsty. A glass of lemonade would be very welcome.'

'Lemonade it is,' said Mr Emberton cheerfully. 'Now sit there Miss Diana, until I return. I shall not be gone long for I do not wish to battle with any of your suitors when I return.'

He decided to get Diana a little something stronger to drink. He poured out a glass of lemonade and added a large measure of arak to it.

'It's a sort of liquorice-flavoured lemonade,' he said on his return. 'Very refreshing.'

Diana took a large gulp and choked. 'It tastes very odd.'

'But very cooling,' he said. 'Was that your father's carriage I saw as I arrived? The old-fashioned thing with the great yellow wheels?'

'That is our travelling carriage,' smiled Diana. 'I fear it is very antiquated. Papa's racing curricle, on the other hand, is bang up to the mark.'

Mr Emberton was turning a plot over in his head. He was beginning to think out a way to turn this so far unsuccessful evening to his advantage.

He realized she was asking him about that wretched elopement and why he had fled without even speaking to her.

He did not want to confess himself afraid of Dantrey so he said seriously, 'I regretted my rash act, Miss Diana. All at once I thought of all the shame and disgrace into which you would be falling by eloping with me. I could not go on with it.

'When I found you were not to be married, I felt such relief. Now I can court the lady as befits her station, that is what I thought. Of course, had you been pressed into an unsuitable marriage, I would have snatched you away from the altar if necessary. But then, there was the sad loss of your mother. I wanted to comfort you, to at least write, but I was afraid I had lost you. My behaviour seems so clumsy now. Please forgive me.'

But he was unable to hear whether Diana forgave him or not for the officer who had been dancing with Ann came up to beg Diana's hand for the next dance. Feeling a surge of confidence because of the effects of the arak in her lemonade and being urged to accept by Mr Emberton who had plans of his own for the next few minutes, Diana rose confidently to her feet and found that this time she was able to dance with ease and even pretend to be enjoying the officer's company, particularly when she danced anywhere near Lord Dantrey.

Lord Dantrey watched Mr Emberton leaving the ballroom and wondered idly where he was going. He decided to take his own leave. He was suddenly weary of the noise and the heat of the ballroom, and if Diana Armitage was hell-bent on throwing herself away on a card sharp, then who was he to stop her?

CHAPTER EIGHT

Very few guests ever left an assembly at the Cock and Feathers until after the very last dance and so the stable staff were all taking their ease in the tap.

Lord Dantrey wondered whether to summon the landlord to find an ostler for him and then decided to walk to the stables and fetch his carriage himself. He had driven himself to the ball and had not even taken a groom, the roads of Berham county being safe from highwaymen and footpads. It was then he saw Mr Emberton gliding stealthily into the darkness of the stables. Lord Dantrey quietly followed him, wondering what he was up to.

A glow of light flickered as Mr Emberton lit an oil lamp and hung it on the stable wall. Lord Dantrey drew back into the shadows.

He saw with amazement that Mr Emberton was proceeding to loosen one of the bolts on the front nearside wheel of what he recognized to be the vicarage carriage. It had been pointed out to him earlier by one of the ostlers. He could not plan to *kill* Diana and her father, thought Lord Dantrey. They would take a nasty tumble when the wheel fell off, unless they were very lucky.

While Mr Emberton bent to his work, Lord Dantrey thought hard. He himself was driving his phaeton, and he thought Mr Emberton was probably the owner of that dreadful phaeton with the great red wheels over there. A phaeton only allowed room for one driver and two slim passengers.

Did Mr Emberton plan to offer to drive Diana home? Did he plan to point out the loose wheel before they found out for themselves?

It was possible.

Lord Dantrey waited, concealed. He did not have very long to wait. Mr Emberton's sabotage was quickly done. He went across the stable and checked the red wheeled phaeton, confirming Lord Dantrey's guess that it was his own.

When he had left, Lord Dantrey moved into the stables. After a few minutes' hard work he had successfully loosened the front offside wheel on Mr Emberton's carriage.

'We'll see what he makes of *that,*' thought Lord Dantrey. After some thought, he assumed that Emberton meant the vicar and his daughter to take a spill, *then* come rushing forward in the fuss and offer to take Diana home. He decided to return to the ballroom. He flirted a great deal with Ann Carter, watching Diana the whole time out of the corner of his eye to see if she showed the slightest sign of interest. But Diana, now very happy and elated, was surrounded by a court of admirers and enjoying her first social success to the full.

The dance wore on into the small hours. At last Lord Dantrey saw the vicar and the squire preparing to leave. Mr Emberton followed them out. Lord Dantrey followed as well.

When he reached the outside of the inn, it was to find the ostlers telling the enraged vicar that one of the wheels had fallen off his carriage when they were harnessing it up. The heavy carriage had keeled right over and the axle had broken. John Summer said gloomily that some idiot must have done it deliberate.

'Then you should ha' been in the stables where you belong,' said the vicar nastily.

'Not in the tap.'

'At least I can drive Miss Diana home while you wait for repairs,' said Mr Emberton. 'Miss Diana is much fatigued and it is not good for her to wait in the night air.'

'Ah, so that *is* the plan,' thought Lord Dantrey.

'Mr Emberton's carriage do be broke as well,' said John Summer with a shrug. 'Same thing. Swung over and crashed into the inn wall. Shivered like matchwood, it did.'

'Fetch the parish constable,' snapped the vicar. 'Was ever a man so plagued! Some lunatic has been loose in the stables.'

Mr Emberton stood and ground his teeth in fury.

The squire shivered in the cold. Lord Dantrey walked up. 'I would be glad to escort Miss Diana home, Mr Armitage. Squire Radford would be glad to be home in bed, I think, and he will act as chaperone, should you have any worries on that head.'

'Course I got worries,' grumbled the vicar. He was about to say more, but the squire, anxious to get home, whispered to him that all would be well.

'But I don't want to stay here, waiting

about till dawn until blacksmith gets out o' bed,' moaned the vicar. 'I don't . . .'

His voice trailed away. One of the inn's chambermaids, Joan, a buxom middle-aged woman, was hanging out of a side window of the inn that overlooked the stables. Her generous breasts bulged over the sill and, as the vicar looked up, she gave him a broad wink.

'As I was sayin',' said the vicar hurriedly, 'all I want is to get you home, Jimmy—and Diana too, o' course. Won't do me no harm to rack up here for the night,' he added, raising his voice.

Jack Emberton was fuming. He did not like spending money, and he was already counting the expense of this evening from his new suit of clothes to his ruined carriage. Added to that, he would now have to pay for a room for the night.

'Perhaps we could share a room, sir,' he said to the vicar in the hope that Mr Armitage would pay his shot.

'No, won't do,' said the vicar crossly, casting a glance up at the chambermaid. 'I snore. Can't bear to sleep with a *man* in the room.'

Lord Dantrey had turned away to talk to

the squire. Mr Emberton said to Diana in a low voice, 'May I call on you tomorrow?'

'Of course,' said Diana. 'We will be most happy to see you.'

Soon Diana found herself seated in Lord Dantrey's high perch phaeton. The little squire sat between her and Lord Dantrey. They were well-wrapped up in carriage rugs and with hot bricks at their feet. Lord Dantrey was content to drive slowly, talking to the squire about his estates and the improvements he hoped to make. Diana was left alone to think about Mr Emberton. He was such a *comfortable* man, but somehow, when she was not with him, she no longer longed to see him again. But surely he would make the ideal husband. Lord Dantrey would most certainly *not* be a good choice for a husband. He would always be off flirting with some silly girl. He made one feel hot and uncomfortable.

And yet . . . he had great charm. Even the normally shrewd squire had obviously fallen victim to it and was chatting away animatedly, his earlier fatigue obviously forgotten.

A red sun was peeping over the horizon as the village of Hopeworth appeared at the end of the road. The whole world was bathed in a fiery red glow. The frost on the hedges and on the long shaggy winter grasses at the side of the road blazed like rubies.

The squire seemed to have forgotten he was supposed to be chaperoning Diana. He offered Lord Dantrey refreshment when they arrived at his cottage *ornée* but Lord Dantrey refused, saying he was anxious to see Miss Diana safely home.

The effects of all she had drunk combined with the fresh air were beginning to make Diana feel sleepy. It was only such a little way to the vicarage. Nothing embarrassing could happen to her. And Lord Dantrey had said he had no intention of repeating any familiarities.

The horses clop-clopped steadily around the village pond which burned like a sheet of flame under the rising sun.

Lord Dantrey had fallen silent. Diana yawned and pulled the fur carriage rug more tightly about her shoulders.

All at once, the sleepy feeling left her and she felt tension invading her body.

The air about her seemed to crackle. His hands holding the reins were relaxed but there was a feeling emanating from him, restless and excited.

The vicarage gates were standing open and he turned the phaeton neatly in through the gate posts.

They came to a stop outside the vicarage. He jumped lightly down and held up his arms to assist Diana from the high perch seat of the phaeton.

She took his hands and leapt down. He held her hands very tightly, looking down into her face. Then he released them only to wind his arms about her and hold her very close.

He had a strange expression on his face, puzzled and anxious. He wanted to kiss her. He wanted to kiss her very much indeed, but was held back from doing so by the memory of the look of disgust she had had on her face the last time he had done so.

'Please,' she said, her voice a little above a whisper. 'Please don't.'

Why couldn't he leave her alone? Because she excited his senses, because she made him drunk. And he still could not bear to think the immense longing and excitement were all on his side.

He took her face gently between his long fingers and bent his mouth to hers.

Diana did not know why it happened, but this time it was very different. Her whole body surrendered to him. His lips moved from her mouth to kiss her closed eyelids and her cold cheeks and then returned to her mouth in a seeking, searching, yearning kiss, bending her body back in his arms and arching over her. Diana wanted that kiss to go on forever, blotting out space and time.

When he raised his lips again for a moment, a sudden alarm bell went off in her head, faint at first but beginning to clamour loudly as he searched for her mouth again.

He had not said a word. He had not murmured one word of love. She was rapidly melting away to nothing in his arms. Her will was being taken away from her and her independence. If she did not escape then soon she would turn into a weak, pitiful, doting creature, waiting for the sound of his step, longing for a kind look, for the pressure of his hand.

She freed her mouth. 'Let me go,' she said in a high, pleading voice. 'Oh, do let me go.'

His hands dropped to his sides. Her wild, wide eyes looked up at him. Then she burst into tears, avoiding his grasp as he would have held her, running away into the house and slamming the door.

'Emberton,' thought Lord Dantrey savagely. 'Always Emberton.'

He turned the problem of Diana Armitage over and over in his mind until he thought he had found a solution.

As his sleepy butler helped him out of his topcoat and took his hat and gloves, Lord Dantrey asked him, 'Chalmers, what is the name of the biggest gossip in Berham county?'

Upset as she was, Diana firmly dried her eyes when she reached the sanctuary of her room and sat down to write to Frederica. She wrote quickly, the quill scratching across the paper. Frederica would read about a very different assembly from the one Diana had just attended. There was very little mention of Lord Dantrey except that she had been obliged to let him drive her home since the wheel of the carriage had come off. She praised Mr Emberton's dancing, charm and looks, as if by writing it all down she could blot out the ever-haunting face of Lord Dantrey. She forced herself to describe the gowns of the ladies and the dress of the gentlemen and all the things that had been served at supper.

At last she sanded the letter and undressed, climbing wearily into bed, putting the aching of her body down to fatigue, for it could have nothing to do with longing. She had drunk too much. She did *not* love Lord Dantrey. In fact, she was absolutely determined not to. And with that thought, she tumbled headlong into sleep.

When she awoke the next day she could hardly believe it was late in the afternoon. The sun was already sliding down the sky, the bare branches of the trees in the garden sending long fingers of shadow into the room. The curtains were drawn back and there was a tray of tea and biscuits beside the bed, mute witness to the fact that Sarah had been in and had decided to let her mistress stay asleep.

Diana rang the bell beside the bed. After some minutes she realized that Sarah was probably out, or flirting with someone at the kitchen door. Well, one could not expect a lady's maid to behave like a lady's maid when the girl was given so many other duties. Diana often thought her father regarded Sarah as *his* personal servant.

Mr Emberton had no doubt called as he

had promised. Lord Dantrey had probably called as well since it was customary for gentlemen to pay their respects to the ladies they had danced with the night before. Finding her asleep, both had probably gone on to call on the Carters where they no doubt had received a rapturous welcome. Diana longed to see Mr Emberton. His easy, friendly manner, his open admiration would be balm to the aching wound that was Lord Mark Dantrey.

She put on her riding habit, wondering whether her very enjoyment in riding was suitable for a young lady in mourning. But Minerva had seen nothing wrong in her going out with the hunt and Minerva was always correct. The shako had been beyond repair but Sarah had tied black silk veiling around the crown of a mannish beaver, transforming it into a suitable riding hat for a lady.

After a brief meal of eggs and tea and toast, Diana went round to the stables and asked John Summer to saddle up Blarney. As usual, John Summer offered to accompany her, not feeling it was quite correct for miss to ride out on her own. But Diana wanted to be alone with her thoughts. Soon her flying figure could be seen vanishing over the horizon. Diana had decided to go in search of the gypsy woman.

Mr Emberton returned from the vicarage earlier, after having failed to see Diana, and suggested to his friend, Peter Flanders, that they might as well cut their losses and return to town.

Mr Flanders studied Mr Emberton out of the corner of his eye. He did not want to go back to St James's so soon. Mr Flanders was well aware that several young men blamed their ruin on having been introduced to Mr Emberton by himself.

'You see, I think she's spoony about Dantrey,' said Jack Emberton, 'although I don't think Dantrey wants *her*. He's set his sights on Ann Carter. I went there before I went to the vicarage and he's sitting by the chimney like a kitchen cat with Mrs Carter and Ann fussing over him.'

'Not like you to get so depressed,' said Mr Flanders. 'Miss Armitage can't be indifferent to you. She *did* try to elope with you. Have you ever considered just going over to the vicarage and getting down on one knee and asking her to marry you? She'll either say

"Yes" or "no". If it's "Yes", then when the vicar asks you your prospects and you tell him you ain't got any, you can hint you can be bought off. If it's "no", then we don't need to waste our time in Hopeworth.'

'You're a downy one, Peter,' said Mr Emberton with a slow smile. 'Simplest way is best, heh? But what if Dantrey calls me out?'

'He won't. Not if the girl says she wants to marry you. Besides, you said he ain't interested in Miss Armitage.'

'True . . . but there's something . . . Never mind. I'll call tomorrow. You come with me and hang about and help me find out when the vicar's away.'

'No need for that. What about that pretty maid you was talking about t'other day. She'll tell you, surely.'

'That she will. Delightful armful of ladybird. If Miss Diana says no, then I'll make sure the maid says yes before I quit the neighbourhood.'

'You ain't thinking of marrying a servant?'

Mr Emberton proceeded to tell Mr Flanders exactly what he meant to do to, and with, Sarah until the two gentlemen were helpless with bawdy laughter.

The squire and the vicar were at that moment seated beside the fire in the squire's cottage. The vicar had gone straight to the squire's after returning from Hopeminster. He had had to ride back since the carriage would need extensive repairs. He had a slightly sheepish look as if he felt the squire could divine what he had been up to during the rest of the night at the inn in Hopeminster.

But the squire only wanted to praise the fine qualities of Lord Dantrey. 'Whatever he may have done in his youth, Charles,' said the squire, 'should not be held against him. He is a fine young man. I am sure Diana is not indifferent to him. He would make a most suitable husband.'

'What of Emberton? She seems to like him as well.'

'Despite what Lady Godolphin said, we really do not know anything of this Emberton. He appears to have means, but we still know nothing of his parentage. He is living with a very weak, shiftless sort of fellow by the name of Flanders. You can always judge a man by the company he keeps, Charles.'

260

'Aye, but I have decided to let Diana have which one she wants, and if she don't want any, then she can stay with me. Fact is, I would miss her.'

'But you would not keep her at home simply because you are lonely?'

'No, I ain't lonely. Terrible thing to say with Mrs Armitage not so long gone. But Diana can do as she pleases.'

'She is still very young. It is not always wise to let a young and headstrong girl do what she wants.'

'Diana's got a good head on her shoulders. Oh, I know it didn't look like it when she was cavorting around London with Dantrey, but she's aged amazing.'

This maturity of Diana's seemed to be borne out when Sarah reported that Miss Diana was over visiting Mrs Jones and had called on several other of the parishioners. The vicar smiled at Sarah as she helped him out of his coat. There was nothing to worry about. Diana had grown up fast.

He did not know that Diana had only recollected her duties after she had failed to find the gypsy.

On the following day, Mr Emberton waylaid Sarah in the village and learned that the vicar had gone over to Hopeminster to see how the repairs to the carriage were getting along. He returned to his own home and dressed in his finest—blue swallowtail coat, doeskin breeches, buff waistcoat, and top boots polished to a mirror shine. He had tried to arrange his black curls into one of the fashionable backcombed styles but could not manage to achieve Lord Dantry's elegance. By the time he had washed his hair—the first time in two months—and dried it and arranged it in its usual casual style, it was already late afternoon.

He rode hard to the vicarage, praying that the vicar was still in Hopeminster. Rose let him in, a fact that disappointed him somewhat, for he had been meaning to steal a kiss from Sarah before he saw Diana.

Diana rose to greet him as he was ushered into the parlour. She was wearing a dark grey gown edged with black and her thick hair was piled in a knot on the top of her head. She looked very elegant and assured and older than her years.

He decided to get the business over with as soon as possible before he lost courage.

'Miss Armitage,' he said, dropping to one knee in front of her. *'Diana.* I fell in love with you the very first time I saw you. I am glad our attempts at an elopement failed for I want the whole world to know that I wish to marry you in the correct and proper way.'

Diana looked down at him in wonder. 'Are you proposing *marriage*, Mr Emberton?'

He rose and took her hands in his. 'Yes,' he said. 'Please say you will do me the very great honour to accept my hand in marriage.'

'Please sit down, Mr Emberton,' said Diana, drawing her hands away. She sat down opposite him and studied him sadly. She was wondering why she felt so miserable. The man of her dreams was proposing marriage to her. She ought to feel wonderful. It could not be because of Lord Dantrey. It *would not* be because of Lord Dantrey.

'Have you spoken to my father?' she asked.

'I had hoped to, but I learn he is in Hopeminster.'

'I think I hear him returning,' said Diana.

Mr Emberton threw himself on his knees again. 'Say yes,' he begged. 'I love you so very much.'

'Yes,' said Diana in a tired little voice. 'I will marry you.'

'Hey, what's this?' cried the vicar from the doorway.

Diana stood up and faced him. 'Papa, Mr Emberton has done me the honour of asking me to marry him and I have accepted.'

'Oh, you have, have you? We'll see about that. Come with me, Mr Emberton.'

Mr Emberton followed the vicar into his study. The vicar sat down beside his desk and Mr Emberton sat down opposite him.

'What were you about,' said the Reverend Charles Armitage, 'to propose to my daughter without asking my permission first?'

Mr Emberton began to relax, as he always did when he was about to trick someone. 'Such was my intention, sir, but when I saw Miss Diana's beauty, I fear I could not restrain myself.'

'Well, to business. She has a fair dowry. I expect you to match it. The lawyer over in Hopeworth will draw up the marriage settlements.'

'I fear I cannot. I have no money.'

The vicar blinked.

'If you have no money, how do you pay the rent of the Wentwater place and turn yourself out so fine?'

'I play the tables.'

'For a living?'

'For my sins, yes.'

' 'Fore George, you're a cool one. After what you have just told me, marriage to my daughter is out of the question.'

'I fear you will break her heart, sir. She loves me very much.'

The vicar sat wrestling with his thoughts. He loved Diana, possibly more than his other daughters. She was the one who could sometimes burrow under his hard, self-centred crust. On the other hand, this Emberton had owned up that he had no money. Another man, a lesser man, would have lied or blustered.

'Sarah!' yelled the vicar loudly, making Mr Emberton jump.

Rose answered his call and the vicar's face fell. Just a look at Sarah's generous bosom and golden curls would, he felt, have cleared his head.

'Fetch Miss Diana,' he growled.

Diana came in, looking so white, so tense, and so miserable that the vicar all at once made up his mind.

'Come and sit down, Diana,' he said gently. 'There is a problem here. Mr Emberton has no money and no prospects.

He earns his living gaming.'

'Papa!'

'Fact. He told me so himself.'

Diana closed her eyes as a great wave of relief swept over her. She would not have to marry him. Papa would not let her. Why on earth had she promised? Perhaps because he wanted her and Lord Dantrey did not. Perhaps because she wanted Lord Dantrey to hear of her engagement and know that his kisses meant nothing.

'I am so very sorry,' she began, turning to Mr Emberton.

'There's nothing to be sorry about,' said the vicar cheerfully. 'He's owned up like a gentleman. So here is what I am going to do. I shall give you both an allowance of £200 a year and you can both stay here with me. Got plenty of room,' said the little vicar with an expansive wave of his arm.

'I am not worthy,' babbled Mr Emberton. 'I am,' his voice dropped dramatically, 'what is known as a *card sharp.*'

'Never too late to mend your ways,' said the vicar.

Mr Emberton reflected bitterly that £200 was the amount with which he usually started an evening's gaming. Of course, he could simply pack up and leave . . .

'I will help you on the path to reform,' said the vicar piously. 'O' course, if there was any question of you not mending your ways, then I have the means to see you do.' He smiled at Mr Emberton but his little shoe button eyes were as hard as flint. For all his size, Mr Emberton was a physical coward. He had visions of this hunting parson, this 'squarson', having him stoned if he ever strayed from the straight and narrow. There was more to this than met the eye. He had fallen into a trap. How could he have been so gullible as to believe Diana Armitage a virgin after she had spent two nights, by her own admission, in Dantrey's company? Of course her father would marry her to *anyone* who asked.

The vicar looked at Diana's white face. 'I know you are shocked, my love, but I have only your happiness in mind. This is the man of your choice and I will see that you have him.'

He rang the bell. 'Fetch brandy,' he said to Rose, 'and champagne for Miss Diana. Bring glasses for yourself and the other servants. We'll have a celebration. Miss Diana is to be wed!'

Mr Emberton felt the net close about him. After half an hour, he was not only surrounded by the celebrating vicarage servants but by a great number of the inhabitants of Hopeworth village, including Squire Radford and his Indian servant, Ram. Mr Emberton saw the vicar take the tall powerful Indian aside and whisper something to him and the Indian turned his large brown eyes in Mr Emberton's direction and gave a little nod. The vicar was obviously rallying his forces. Mr Emberton was going to be made to change his ways. He contemplated a flight to London, but in London there were all the powerful Armitage in-laws.

'I do not like this at all, Charles,' said the squire as soon as he was able to have a quiet word with the vicar. 'You say this man is a confessed card sharp. Do you hope to keep him on the path of righteousness by *threatening* him?'

'Don't think I'll need to,' said the vicar cheerfully. 'Love of a good woman and all that.'

'Now, that is a myth,' said the squire severely. 'Once a card sharp, always a . . .'

'Pooh, you say Dantrey's reformed and yet

you refuse to take the word of an upstanding fellow who has confessed the error of his ways.'

'I feel uneasy,' said the squire. 'I only wonder what Dantrey will make of this!'

Diana was glad when she finally retreated to her room. She sat for a long time by the window, wondering what her life would be like with Jack Emberton. That offer of her father's of £200 a year would have seemed a very generous amount before she had gone to London to meet Lord Dantrey. But she now knew that gentlemen like Mr Emberton would consider that enough for an evening's pleasure. Still, he must love her very much indeed to tell her father the truth and promise to reform. Mr Emberton had been left alone with her briefly to say goodnight. He had taken her in his arms and kissed her. His mouth had been hot and wet and he had smelled of sweat. She was glad when the embrace was over although it seemed to have cheered her fiancé who had looked down at her, smiling slowly in a way she did not like, and saying, 'This might not be so bad a bargain after all.' What had he meant by that? Someone else's lust was acceptable, thought Diana miserably, if it created an answering lust in one's own body. But Mr Emberton's embrace had left her feeling frightened and sick. She tried to concentrate on all her dreams of friendship and companionship but they crumbled before the memory of the hot look in Mr Emberton's eyes.

There was a furtive scuffling and giggling in the corridor. Sarah! She was surely not taking one of her country swains upstairs!

Diana opened the door and looked out.

She held up a candle and looked along the corridor. Sarah's unmistakable giggle was coming from her father's room.

Diana turned and walked shakily back into her room. She sat for a long time in a chair by the window, her thoughts in a turmoil. She felt young and lost and alone. All at once, she began to cry for her mother. Great wrenching sobs shook her body as she longed for the love and warmth and security that Mrs Armitage had never given her.

The news of Miss Diana Armitage's engagement spread from the village of Hopeworth in ever widening ripples all over Berham county. They met up with the ripples of gossip about Mr Emberton's unsavoury background carefully spread by Lord Dantrey's servants until the whole thing grew into a tidal wave and descended on Osbadiston Hall, about the same time as Mr Fane descended from his carriage to pay a visit on Lord Dantrey.

He found his friend in his library, hotly cross-questioning his butler.

'Welcome,' said Lord Dantrey in an abstracted way as his friend walked into the room. 'I will be with you in a minute. Now, Chalmers, you tell me that Mr Armitage *knows* that Mr Emberton is a card sharp and yet is allowing the marriage to go ahead?'

'That is the case,' said the butler, Chalmers. 'It seems that the vicar is determined to allow Miss Diana to wed because Mr Emberton has promised to mend his ways.'

'Very well, Chalmers, you may go.'

'What was all that about?' asked Mr Fane when the butler had left the room.

'*That* was all about the fair Miss Armitage. Mr Emberton proposed marriage and told the vicar that he, Emberton, is a wastrel and a card sharp. The good vicar was evidently so impressed by the man's honesty that he not only gave him his daughter but offered him an allowance, just when I thought I had put a spoke in that particular wheel.'

'How?'

'I did not want to see any girl being misled by Emberton and so I got my servants to spread the news of his doubtful character about the district. Unfortunately, all that did was to reinforce public opinion in the view that Emberton is a reformed character. By the time *my* gossip got about, the vicarage gossip of Emberton's confession was already abroad. Perhaps he really loves her.'

'Well, she must love him,' said Mr Fane reasonably, 'else she wouldn't have said she would marry him.'

'Do you think so?'

'Stands to reason,' said Mr Fane awkwardly. Lord Dantrey's face looked so white and set.

'I cannot believe it,' muttered Lord Dantrey. 'I *will* not believe it until I have seen them together.'

'I did not realize you loved her yourself,' said Mr Fane.

'I don't know if I do. She infuriates me. But she's too good to be tied to the likes of Emberton.'

'The way I see it,' said Mr Fane, 'there's

nothing to be done at present. Leave fellows like Emberton alone and they'll soon emerge in their true colours. What you need is some other girl to take your mind off Miss Armitage. What about this Miss Carter you wrote to me about?'

'You shall meet her,' said Lord Dantrey. 'I promised to take you along to one of her mother's dreadful salons. I accepted on our behalf yesterday.'

'There you are then. That will take your mind off things. And you did promise me some sport.'

'Forgive me. I am a very bad host. You have just arrived and I have not even allowed you time to wash and change. Miss Armitage is a silly girl and all I will do is make a fool of myself if I become embroiled in her troubles.'

A week later, Mr Emberton had the honour of driving his bride-to-be, Miss Diana Armitage, to Mrs Carter's salon in her father's racing curricle, his own carriage having proved to be beyond repair.

It was the first time since the night of their engagement that they had been alone together. Diana was wearing the pale green carriage dress she had worn in London when she had gone driving with him, only this time she wore a magnificent sable lined mantle over it, a present from Minerva. She wore a black hat with a narrow brim. Black silk ribbon was wound around the crown and fell in two streamers down her back. Long emerald earrings swung against her cheeks. 'At least I can pawn her clothes if I need to marry the jade,' thought Mr Emberton bitterly. He was still furious over being trapped. Most of all he was furious at Diana's reaction to his embrace. How dare she act so virginal when she had already given Dantrey her favours.

He had seriously thought of escape and had gone so far as to ask the Wentwater servants to look out his trunks. But they had reported that fact immediately to the vicarage and the vicar had promptly turned up, flanked by John Summer and Ram, demanding to know why he was leaving.

He had laughed it off, saying that he was looking out his old clothes to parcel them up and give them away. The vicar had cheerfully said he would take the clothes for the Poor Fund and so he had had to part with some of his clothes to give support to the lie.

The feeling that he had been well and truly gulled persisted and grew and rankled as Miss Diana sat bolt upright beside him, saying never a word.

It was then that he realized he could try to make her cry off. Why should he be saddled with Haymarket ware? Dantrey had said nothing since the announcement of the engagement. He was probably laughing his head off at the idea of some other man having to take his used goods.

He could accuse Diana of sleeping with Dantrey and during the surely blazing row that would ensue she would tell him she did not want to marry him. But of *course* she wanted to marry him. What man in his right mind would want her now?

But apart from myself, Dantrey and her family, no one else knows, he thought. He turned to Diana to say something nasty but the cold severity of her profile gave him pause. But wait a bit. He had something. There was light at the end of the tunnel. For the first time he saw a way to extricate himself from the trap he was in.

But before he did that, why not try to sample some of the goods that had been given so freely to Dantrey? He stopped his team and turned to Diana.

'Alone at last,' he said with a wide smile.

Diana drew her fur mantle closely about her. 'Please drive on, Mr Emberton,' she said in a tight little voice. 'You should not leave my father's horses standing in this weather.'

He dropped the reins and seized her in his arms, forcing his mouth down on hers and thrusting his tongue between her teeth. Then he let out a muffled scream as she bit down hard on his tongue. The horses plunged and reared. He cursed and raised his hand to strike her but then he heard the sound of another carriage coming along the road behind him, and so he set the horses in motion, muttering, 'You will not dare behave thus after we are married.'

How horrible he has turned out to be, thought Diana, feeling tears pricking behind her eyelids. How disgusting! I can't marry him. Papa is now so proud of his generosity and magnanimity that he will not want the engagement to end. All he cares about at the moment is Sarah. How could any girl . . . ? A man old enough to be her father. *My* father, dear God. Is there something up with me? Does everyone else roll around like mating animals?

Mrs Carter's house was the very latest in modern building design. It boasted delicate balconies, verandahs, cupolas and classical mouldings, bow fronts, hooded windows, and generous doorways. The stucco was however painted an ice cream pink so that instead of merging tastefully with the landscape it stood out like a pimple.

Everything inside was new and glittering. There were walls with striped flocked paper and backless sofas upholstered in striped silk. Huge ornate marble candelabra on marble stands dotted the room, the candles lit because of the darkness of the day. Vast looking glasses reflected the company several times. Mrs Carter was very fond of fat cherubs. They sported over the moulding on the fireplace and hung from the cornices. They leaned down from the painted ceiling with pouting ruby lips and two kneeling ones held up a centre table of malachite. The colour scheme was pink and white. Ann too was in pink and white, a ravishingly pretty gown of near transparent muslin. She tripped forward to greet Diana with both hands held out in welcome. The welcome was genuine. Ann felt that Lord Dantrey would now propose to her with Diana safely engaged to another man. Mrs Carter had not wanted to invite Mr Emberton but was afraid not to since no one else in the county had even considered snubbing him. A secretive card sharp was one thing, a self-confessed one set on reform and engaged to one of the Armitage girls was another.

Diana left Mr Emberton's side and went to speak to the Chumleys, accepting their congratulations on her engagement.

Then there were more congratulations to accept. She numbly thanked everyone with a forced smile while all the while she became more determined to tell Mr Emberton she could not marry him.

Mrs Carter's salon, as she liked to call it, was held between the front and back drawing rooms on the ground floor, with a room being set aside for cards. A small orchestra was playing tinny Elizabethan tunes and servants circulated with glasses of punch. The punch was Mrs Carter's own invention. Mr Emberton took one sip and then raised his eyebrows. It had a kick like a mule although it tasted very sweet and innocuous.

After several glasses of the stuff, he began to relax. He would find a way out of this mess. Lord Dantrey's tall figure walked into the room, followed by Mr Fane. He proceeded to introduce his friend all round to everyone in the company with notable exceptions of Diana and Mr Emberton. Mr Emberton had several more glasses of punch and his feeling of euphoria slowly gave way to one of anger. Who did Dantrey think he was? He should have been slapping him on the back and wishing him well. The room tilted a little and then righted itself. Through an alcoholic haze Mr Emberton saw Lord Dantrey walk up to Diana, who had been standing alone by the window.

He found Ann Carter standing at his elbow. 'It is disgusting,' he said to her fiercely, 'at least I thought they would have the decency to keep apart.'

'Who? Lord Dantrey and Diana?' asked Ann, round-eyed.

Mr Emberton finally saw a way out of his predicament and decided to seize it with both hands. 'I must talk to someone,' he said sorrowfully. 'I have been most shamefully duped.'

'You can tell me,' said Ann, scenting a scandal. Although she was fully aware of her mother's beady eye on her, she pulled Mr

Emberton a little away from the other guests. 'Now tell me,' she said eagerly.

'I found out after I had proposed to Diana,' said Mr Emberton, 'that she had spent a week with Lord Dantrey in town, dressed as a *man!*'

'No!'

'Yes, and worse than that, she even spent a night at his house at Osbadiston Hall.'

'But how did you find out all this?'

'She told me,' said Mr Emberton. 'She threw it in my face. Now I must marry her for Dantrey will not.'

'Oooh! But no one can make you marry her.'

'Mr Armitage has threatened to have me killed an I do not. *That* is why he spread that malicious slander about me being a card sharp so that should a hint of any of the scandal come out, people would think a low type such as I must have known of it and that I must have been *paid* to marry the girl.'

Ann drew a deep breath. She did not want this scandal to get about. If Mrs Carter found out that Lord Dantrey had spent a week in London with Diana Armitage then she would not let her, Ann, marry him. And Ann wanted very much to marry Lord

Dantrey. She liked his looks, his title, and his fortune. She was not in the slightest shocked that he had spent the night with a woman. All men were like that. Mama had told her so and Mama was never wrong.

She began to edge away from Mr Emberton. He caught her arm. 'What am I to do, Miss Carter?'

Mrs Carter strode up, glaring. 'Mama,' bleated Ann, 'I think that Mr Emberton is a trifle *foxed.*' Her mother drew her away.

Jack Emberton stood clenching and unclenching his fists. He had another glass of punch. What was Dantrey saying to Diana?

'I am not going to congratulate you on your marriage,' he was saying. 'What made you do such a thing?'

'Oh, why does one usually accept a proposal of marriage?'

'To teach me a lesson?'

'You are vain. I did not think of you.'

'You did not think of me,' he mimicked. 'You! My dear girl, you responded to my embrace like a woman in love.'

Diana's face flamed. 'I respond to Mr Emberton's embrace like a woman in love,' she lied.

Lord Dantrey suddenly had a picture of Diana locked in Emberton's arms and a red mist rose before his eyes.

'Slut!' he said.

Diana drew her hand to slap his face but he snatched it and drew her close until they were standing close together, glaring at each other.

'Aye, well you may stare,' shouted Jack Emberton, his voice loud and harsh and ugly.

Silence fell on the room.

'Look at the love birds,' jeered Mr Emberton. Lord Dantrey dropped Diana's hand and strode towards him. Mr Fane caught Lord Dantrey and held him back.

'I have to take your leavings,' howled Mr Emberton. 'She,' he said, pointing to Diana, 'she taunted me with the fact she had dressed as a man and spent the night with Dantrey and then she went off with him to London. They stayed at Limmer's together. Now the vicar is forcing me to marry her.'

Lord Dantrey shrugged off Mr Fane's grip and smashed his fist hard into Emberton's jeering face. Mr Emberton flew back sending furniture and glasses crashing about him. Ladies screamed and fainted. The gentlemen crowded round, delighted to have this boring day enlivened by a first class mill.

Lord Dantrey bent down and seized Mr Emberton by the cravat and pulled him to his feet. 'You would not hit a wounded man,' screamed Mr Emberton, blood flowing from his nose. Lord Dantrey drew back his fist and delivered a straight right to Mr Emberton's chin. Mr Emberton fell backwards and stretched his length unconscious on the floor.

Mrs Carter was screaming and screaming. Diana took one horrified look about the room and then ran from the house. She took the first horse she could find in the stables and rode off as hard as she could, her skirts hitched up around her legs. Her one thought was to get home, find some money and escape. This was too big a scandal to ever live down.

She dismounted before she reached the vicarage and led the horse gently to the stables, so as not to rouse anyone in the house.

Then she saddled up her mare, Blarney, before going into the house and creeping quietly up the stairs. There was a clatter of dishes and the sound of laughter from the kitchens. She went to the twins' room and selected a suit of clothes, thankful that her two brothers had reached that dandified stage of life when they had more clothes than any two young men could possibly need. She packed a saddle bag with clean linen and found the money she had saved, nearly intact, since she had spent little on her last escapade.

Once again, she savagely cropped her hair and threw the tresses into the fire. Then she took a length of linen and bound her breasts as flat as possible.

All this seemed to take ages but in fact it had only taken her under half an hour. Before she left, she crept quietly into her mother's room and took a little painted miniature of her from the wall.

Once safely outside the house she swung herself up into the saddle and rode off, never once turning around.

CHAPTER NINE

When Frederica was summoned to the principal's office in the seminary for young ladies her first thought was that she was in trouble. Had they found the candle she had carefully hidden under her pillow so that she could read at night?

School had not turned out to be so very bad after all. She had made friends with a cheerful bouncing girl of her own age called Bessie Bradshaw. Bessie was as outgoing as Frederica was introverted and the one complemented the other.

By the time Frederica pushed open the door of the office she decided it must be the candle and wondered whether to tell the truth or to lie and say she did not know how it got there.

The principal was a fussy faded lady. She was not alone in the room. A young man stood looking out of the window, his back towards Frederica.

'Ah, Frederica,' said the principal. 'I have told your brother it is customary to let us know in advance when any of the girls are expecting visitors. You may use my room for ten minutes.'

The young man at the window turned and Frederica gave a gasp of surprise.

'Is anything the matter?' demanded the principal.

'No-no, ma'am,' faltered Frederica. 'My brother has grown so tall, I hardly recognized him.'

'Very well,' said the principal. 'Ten minutes and no more.'

Frederica waited until the door had closed.

'Diana!' she exclaimed. 'Why are you dressed like that?'

'Oh, Freddie,' sighed Diana, 'I have brought distress on our family. I am in such a mess.'

'Tell me,' urged Frederica, 'and I will see what I can do.'

'I don't know if I can manage to tell you all in ten minutes,' said Diana, 'but I will try.' She proceeded to tell her amazed sister everything that had happened.

When she had finished Frederica clasped her hands and said, 'Only tell me what to do to help you.'

'There is nothing you *can* do, Freddie,' sighed Diana. 'I am come to say goodbye. I think I will go to London and call on Lady Godolphin and ask her to help me find some work. She will not be shocked, you know. It is no use going to Minerva or Annabelle or any of the others. They would only tell father and I would have to return to Hopeworth and I couldn't bear to face anyone after all the scandal.'

'But I think you love this Lord Dantrey,' said Frederica.

'That does not matter. One thing is very clear, Freddie, and that is that he does not love me. Oh, dear, I hear that woman returning.'

'At least write to me,' begged Frederica, hanging onto her sleeve.

Diana gave her sister a fierce hug. 'I *will* write, Freddie,' she whispered.

She made her bow to the principal who had just entered the room, and then left.

Frederica ran upstairs and looked out of the landing window onto the courtyard below. Diana sat on her mare, Blarney, her head bowed. Tears were running down her face when she finally raised her head and set off down the drive at a canter.

Frederica turned from the window and found herself staring at her own reflection in the glass. Her dark hair hung in distressed wisps from under her cap and her large no-colour eyes stared wistfully back at her. She had a picture of Diana when she was happy, vital, beautiful and very much alive. Diana was made to fall in love and live happily ever after, an enviable state to which Frederica was convinced she herself could never aspire. Better that her own lovers remained between the covers of her books where they could not condemn or find fault with this one Armitage failure, this one daughter who had inherited neither looks, nor charm, nor grace. She gave a little sigh and thought of Diana, vulnerable and alone in the world.

'It's just not *fair*,' muttered Frederica. 'Something must be done to stop her.' She sat down on the stairs and thought hard. Then she ran down to the deserted school library and found a pen and some paper.

She took a deep breath, pulled the paper towards her and began to write. 'Dear Lord Dantrey . . .'

Two days later Lady Godolphin was

awakened by the sound of one of her servants scratching at the door. She groaned and cursed. Why this morning of all mornings had one of her normally discreet staff decided to behave badly?

'Grrmph,' said a sleepy voice from the other pillow.

'Go to sleep, Arthur,' said Lady Godolphin to Colonel Brian. ' 'Tis only some stupid servant.'

The scratching persisted.

Lady Godolphin adjusted her scarlet wig and tied the ribbons of her nightcap more securely under her chin, swung her legs out of bed and waddled to the door.

She opened the door a crack and glared at Mice, her butler.

'What are you about, you great lummox, waking me at dawn?' she demanded.

'It is one o'clock in the afternoon,' said Mice in injured tones.

'That's dawn, you fool.'

'Mr David Armitage has been waiting downstairs for the past four hours, my lady. He said not to wake you but the young man seems in some distress . . .'

'Oh, lor',' groaned Lady Godolphin. 'Very well.'

'What was all that about?' mumbled Colonel Brian from the bed.

'Never mind,' said Lady Godolphin, her voice muffled as she pulled a petticoat over her head without undoing the tapes. 'We're cross lovers, that's what we are Arthur.'

'My love, how could I ever be cross with you?'

'Well, that's what the poet said. Pair o' cross lovers. 'Course they was foreigners, although one lot belonged to the Montagus and they're as English as roast beef. Not feeling any pangs of remorse, are you, my duck?'

'No, my angel, my fall from grace was a marvellous thing. Let us be married as quickly as possible.'

'Oh, *Arthur!*' squealed Lady Godolphin, wrenching off her petticoat with such force that her wig went over one ear. She threw herself on the bed.

'My lady will be with you presently,' said Mice to Diana. He raised his eyes at the sound of creaking bed which was coming from upstairs. 'Perhaps in another half hour.'

He was optimistic. It was another two

hours before Lady Godolphin finally put in an appearance. Her conscience smote her when she saw Diana's white, tear-stained face.

'Back in man's clothes again,' said Lady Godolphin when the servants had served them with cakes and wine and left.

'Now it's no use a-crying, Diana. You'd best tell me all.'

Lady Godolphin listened to Diana's tale of woe with horror. She was proud of the success of the Armitage girls. How society would laugh and snigger over this appalling piece of gossip.

'And so,' ended Diana, 'I thought perhaps you might be able to help me find work. I would rather work as a man. I am quite good with horses.'

'Tish. You must let me think. It's no use me moralizing and preaching because I ain't a saint. I was married before I started any fun and games; and a married woman can get away with a lot. If this Dantrey was as mad as you say he was and hit this Emberton fellow, then it stands to reason he must have a *tendre* for you.'

Diana sadly shook her cropped head.

'To think I was so misled by that Mr

Emberton,' wailed Lady Godolphin. 'Let me think.'

She put her chin on her hand and gazed into the fire. She knew what she should do and that was write to Charles Armitage and tell him his daughter was safe. But that would mean Diana would have to go home in disgrace. The family would have to get together and raise an enormous dowry, for no man would want her now unless he was paid to marry her. Lady Godolphin silently cursed the late Mrs Armitage. If she had not been so self-indulgent with her drugs and potions then she would be on this earth and doing her maternal duty. At least Sally, the maid, was the only servant in the house who knew that Diana Armitage and David Armitage were not two different people, and Sally would not talk.

Lady Godolphin rang the bell. 'Arthur will know what to do,' she said firmly.

'Arthur?'

'Colonel Brian. We are to be married and you are the first to know, Diana.'

Diana gave Lady Godolphin her heartfelt congratulations, but trembled inside, wondering what Colonel Brian would think of the scandal.

The Colonel, when he arrived, seemed to take it all in his stride as if young debutantes dressed as men and running away from home were part and parcel of everyday life.

'I have a cousin,' he said, 'who was very wild in her youth. She is now married and living in Boston in America. I suggest we buy Diana a passage to America and I will furnish her with letters of introduction. She may start a new life. My cousin, Jane Croxley, is kind and warm-hearted.'

'But to send her all that way!' moaned Lady Godolphin.

'It need not be forever,' said the colonel. 'After a few years when the scandal has died down, she may return.'

'What think you of this plan?' Lady Godolphin asked Diana.

'It is very kind of you, Colonel Brian,' said Diana in a low voice. All at once she knew she could not bear to return to Hopeworth, to live with her shame, to hear of Lord Dantrey's marriage to Ann Carter. 'Only please do not tell anyone until after I have left.'

Lady Godolphin shook her heavy head. 'It would be too cruel to keep them waiting. It will take time to arrange your passage. I will send one of my servants down to Hopeworth this day to say you have already left and another to your sisters. You may as well stay dressed the way you are.' Lady Godolphin ran a critical eye over Diana's clothes. 'Or better than you are,' she amended. 'Colonel Brian will see to it that you have a new suit of clothes and some decent cravats.'

Lady Godolphin and Colonel Brian threw themselves into the plot with great energy. The Colonel went off to find out about ships to America and Lady Godolphin sat down and composed a letter to the Reverend Charles Armitage.

'I left it too late,' said Lord Dantrey savagely a week later to his friend, Mr Tony Fane. 'She has sailed for America.'

He kicked the logs in the grate and stared down moodily into the leaping flames.

'Gone just like that!' exclaimed Mr Fane. 'It surely takes longer than a week to arrange a passage.'

'Lady Godolphin wrote to Mr Armitage to say she had already left. Some old lover of hers, Colonel Brian, arranged that Diana should stay with a cousin of his in Boston.'

'Seems like a sensible arrangement.'

'It seems like an unnecessary arrangement,' said Lord Dantrey bitterly. 'Did I not terrify that idiot Emberton into saying he had made the whole story up out of jealousy? He will not dare open his mouth now. I told Armitage that and he just sighed heavily and said he would write to Diana in Boston and tell her to come home.'

'That's good news,' said Mr Fane. 'All you have to do is wait for her to return. You could write to her yourself.'

'By the time she gets my letter, she could be married to some Boston bumpkin.'

'Perhaps she might have said something about you to Lady Godolphin before she left. *That* would be a little comfort.'

'Perhaps. I will go to town and speak to her anyway. Do you come with me?'

'Of course. Don't want to stay here in the country on my own.'

Chalmers, the butler, opened the door. 'Mrs Carter and Miss Ann Carter,' he said.

Lord Dantrey did not even look round.

'We are not at home, Chalmers,' he said. 'Now, or at any other time.'

When Frederica was told a gentleman was waiting to see her, her heart soared. Diana!

Perhaps she had decided to stay. Perhaps she was returning to Hopeworth.

But it was the stocky figure of her father who came forward to greet her.

'Papa!' said Frederica nervously, wondering whether to ask about Diana.

'Just thought I would call to see how you go on,' said the vicar cheerfully.

Frederica's heart rose. He would not look so cheerful if Diana were still missing.

'Diana is well, I hope, Papa?' she timidly ventured.

The vicar's face fell. 'As to Diana,' he said, 'Lady Godolphin has made a right mull of things. Seems she's packed her off to some relative o' Colonel Brian's in America. Oh, you won't have heard of the scandal.'

'I did. Diana wrote to me,' said Frederica, not wanting to say that Diana had called in person.

'It seems that Lord Dantrey made Emberton tell everyone he was lying so there was no reason for Diana to leave at all. Well, well. At least there isn't a stain on her character and she can return any time she likes. I have written to her. Lady Godolphin sent me the address.'

Frederica now wished she had not posted

that letter to Lord Dantrey. She had not wanted to give it to the principal since all letters addressed to anyone outside one's own immediate family were usually read. It had taken her days before she had managed to slip it to the post boy.

'Fact is,' said the vicar, 'there's been a want o' care in your upbringing.'

'Minerva looked after us all very well, and Mama, too,' said Frederica loyally.

'Aye, well, it's you who are my concern now, my chuck. I'll tell you a secret. You are to have a new mama.'

'So-so soon?'

'It would not be fitting for me to get married before the year of mourning is over,' said the vicar righteously.

'Who is the lady, Papa?'

'Well, hah, don't you see,' said the vicar shuffling his feet. 'It's Sarah.'

'*Sarah!* The *maid!*'

'Don't come those hoity-toity airs with me, miss. Sarah will do very well. Ain't you going to congratulate me?'

'Congratulations, Papa,' said Frederica faintly.

'A fine thing for you to have a mama, heh?'

'Yes, Papa.'

'Don't look so miserable then.'

'It is only that I sorely miss Diana. What will she think about Sarah?'

'Don't matter what she thinks.'

'Minerva?'

'See here, miss, I ain't told Minerva or the others. They won't be living with us but you will. So not a word until I'm ready to announce the wedding.'

After her father had left, Frederica ran to her room and lay face down on the bed. The world had fallen apart. She *would not* live at the vicarage with Sarah. She would run away from school.

Lord Dantrey left Lady Godolphin's feeling angry and wretched. There seemed no doubt that Diana had sailed. All the way to London he had hoped to find her still there. He returned to the lodgings in Jermyn Street which he was sharing with Mr Fane. His post lay on the table just inside the door. There was a large parcel of letters which had been tied up and forwarded from Hopeminster.

He sifted through them, finally carrying the packet from Hopeminster into the living room and slitting it open. One letter addressed to him in a round feminine hand seemed to leap out at him from all the others. She had written to him after all.

He opened it quickly and scanned the contents. It was not from Diana. Frederica! That was the youngest who was at school. He read it again carefully. Frederica had written to tell him that Diana had called at the school and was on her way to stay with Lady Godolphin. Frederica begged him to help 'because I am sure she loves you,' she had written in a round schoolgirlish hand.

'Too late,' thought Lord Dantrey ruefully.

Lady Godolphin ran screeching and whooping through her mansion like a Red Indian. She erupted into the library where the colonel was sitting beside the fire. 'Arthur!' she shrieked. 'I just had a letter from Charles Armitage. It's all right and tight. Dantrey made Emberton tell everyone he made the whole thing up so Diana can go home and she don't need to go to 'Merica.'

'That is wonderful news. Come and kiss me, my love.'

'In a minute, Arthur. I must find Diana and tell her the news.'

"Kiss me first.'

'Oh, very well, Oh, *Arthur* . . .'

'I wouldn't go in there if I were you, Mr Armitage,' said Mice as Diana stood with her hand on the handle of the library door.

'Oh, dear,' said Diana, retreating. It was very awkward living with such a pair of elderly and energetic lovebirds, she thought. 'Will you tell Lady Godolphin when you can, Mice, that I am going out for a walk.'

'It is not my place, sir, to wonder what is going on,' said Mice severely, 'but I do know you is not supposed to go out of the house.'

'I am only going around the square,' said Diana coldly. 'Please let me past.'

Mice hesitated and then decided there was nothing he could do. He was not going into that library until summoned. There were some sights a man of his delicate sensibility could not stomach. If Mr Armitage wanted to walk around the square there was nothing he, Mice, could do about it.

Diana had only meant to take a short stroll but the sun was shining high above the chimney pots. It was the first real spring day after such a long winter. It had been dreadful being cooped up for so long. Her heart ached for Lord Dantrey but she thought that ache would disappear as soon as she set sail and put as many miles between them as possible. Often she thought he was haunting her. Her mind was full of him. She could hear his voice in her head, feel the touch of his lips on her mouth. She decided to take a walk in the Park.

It was almost like being back in the country again, she thought wistfully. Did father still hunt? Or had the weight of the disgrace she had brought on the family sent him into seclusion?

'I hate these men's clothes,' she thought suddenly, as she watched all the pretty debuntantes in the carriages promenading along Rotten Row. 'When I get to America I will burn them.'

Colonel Brian had obtained a passage for her on the *Mary Jane* which was to sail from Bristol in two weeks' time. Two more weeks of waiting.

Lord Dantrey drove his phaeton down the Row, occasionally nodding to various acquaintances. Beside him sat Mr Fane. 'So that is that,' said Lord Dantrey. 'That letter from Frederica Armitage only made matters worse. I should never have left Diana alone for a moment. I should have followed her from that wretched *salon* and proposed marriage on the spot.'

'She has not fallen off the edge of the world, you know,' said Mr Fane. 'It ain't flat. Nothing to stop you going to America. You won't be that much behind her. Can't expect her to marry the minute she steps off the boat.'

'She might marry *on* the boat,' said Lord Dantrey gloomily. 'If she could find a horror like Emberton attractive, then it stands to reason . . . *Hey, you!*'

'What's the matter?' asked Mr Fane. A slim young man had nearly jumped a foot in the air as Lord Dantrey had shouted and then had started to run away through the trees.

'Hold my horses,' yelled Lord Dantrey, leaping down.

Diana had not seen him. She had only heard his shout. She dared not turn around. It could be Mr Emberton. She heard someone pounding after her and ran harder. Her hat fell off her head and rolled away unheeded across the grass.

Lord Dantrey put on a great spurt of speed and then dived and brought her down with a flying tackle and they both rolled into the centre of a clump of bushes with a great snapping and splintering of twigs.

Diana struggled and rolled over. 'You,' she gasped.

'Yes, me,' said Lord Dantrey passionately, if ungrammatically. 'Kiss me.'

And Diana did, so fiercely and so well that neither of them heard the crowd who had been searching for 'the two coves chasing each other' pass by, leaving them unnoticed.

'I thought you had gone,' said Lord Dantrey at last. 'I thought you were on your way to America. I was about to follow you.'

'You love me,' said Diana in a wondering voice.

'Of course I do, you widgeon.'

'But you can't marry me now,' wailed Diana. 'Everyone will say you had to.'

'All is well. Mr Emberton apologized to everyone and said he had made the whole thing up.'

'Well, I must admit that is very handsome of him. I would not have expected him to . . . Ah, you persuaded him.'

'With my fists. Kiss me again.'

'Someone will see us.'

'No one can see us. We're right in the middle of these bushes. Kiss me.'

'Yes, my lord,' said Diana meekly.

'Mark.'

'Mark what?'

'My name is Mark and are you going to kiss me or not?'

'Yes, Mark.'

After a few moments he asked, 'Why did you promise to marry that villain, Emberton?'

'Because you kissed me and did not say you loved me.'

'Fool. Me, not you.'

He kissed her passionately over and over again until they were both hot and dizzy. 'What is this?' he asked, his hand under her coat.

'An old sheet,' giggled Diana. 'I had to bind my breasts.'

'You will wear the best gowns from now on and you will let that poor shorn head of yours grow a proper crop of hair.'

'You are going to bully me. You are going to tell me what to do and what to wear.'

'Exactly. I am going to indulge in a positive orgy of kissing and *you* are going to indulge *me.*'

An hour later the shaky, dazed couple emerged from the bushes and strolled back to Lady Godolphin's arm in arm.

Her ladyship fell upon them as soon as they came through the door, gasping, 'Where have you been. How *could* you. I have just had a letter from your father and there is *no* scandal and . . .'

'It is all right, Lady Godolphin,' smiled Lord Dantrey. 'Everything is wonderful. We are to be married.'

'God be thanked!' said Lady Godolphin.

Lord Dantrey took Diana in his arms and kissed her.

Mice had felt, after almost a lifetime in service in Lady Godolphin's household, that he was inured to shock. But the sight of two men passionately kissing each other right in Lady Godolphin's hall was too much for him. He reeled down to his pantry and drank a massive measure of brandy before his hands stopped shaking.

They were all gathered at Lady Godolphin's the next week to celebrate Diana's engagement; all the sisters, the in-laws, the vicar and Squire Radford, Colonel Brian and Mr. Fane.

Frederica could only be glad that her father had shown some good taste in not producing Sarah. That bombshell had still to be dropped.

She had given up her plans for running away from school once she had heard of Diana's engagement and the end of the scandal. Diana would know what to do about Sarah.

But Diana seemed to have passed into another world where no one existed for her but Lord Dantrey. Frederica decided gloomily she would have to run away after all. She could not bear the idea of having Sarah as a stepmother.

'I've done very well,' said the vicar, much puffed up in his own conceit. 'No one can say I did not do the best for my daughters. Why, I bet you I could marry Frederica off to a duke!'

Everyone laughed, except Frederica. 'With Sarah as stepmother,' she thought sadly, 'I will be lucky if anyone wants to marry me!'

Diana looked out of her rosy world and saw the shadow on Frederica's face. 'I do not think Freddie is happy,' she whispered to Lord Dantrey.

'That will never do,' he said. 'Do you know she wrote to me and told me you loved me?'

'As I do . . . so very much,' said Diana, and, as he smiled down into her eyes, she forgot about Frederica and everything else except the man standing beside her.

'What are we doing in *York* of all places,' grumbled Mr Peter Flanders.

'We're keeping out of the road until the storm dies down,' said Mr Emberton. 'A pox on that Armitage girl. I'll get even with her one day, see if I don't.'

'Look out!' cried Mr Flanders. 'You're about to walk under a ladder. That's unlucky, you know.'

'Don't be silly. You sound just like Diana Armitage with her curst cats and her damned gypsies.'

Mr Emberton shouldered his way roughly under the lamplighter's ladder. The lamplighter let out a hoarse cry of warning.

Too late.

His can of whale oil upended and cascaded down on Mr Emberton's head.

And as he staggered along the street, wiping his eyes, and cursing Mr Flanders who was dancing beside him, chattering with laughter, a black cat slunk out of a doorway and crept across his path.

The publishers hope that this Large Print Book has brought you pleasurable reading. Each title is designed to make the text as easy to see as possible. G. K. Hall Large Print Books are available from your library and your local bookstore. Or you can receive information on upcoming and current Large Print Books by mail and order directly from the publisher. Just send your name and address to:

G. K. Hall & Co.
70 Lincoln Street
Boston, Mass. 02111

or call, toll-free:

1-800-343-2806

A note on the text
Large print edition designed by
Fred Welden.
Composed in 16 pt Plantin
on an EditWriter 7700
by Cheryl Yodlin of G.K. Hall Corp.